I0537389

THE GEMINI RISING ROCKIN'MACHINE

BOOK THREE: BIG TIME LOVE & BOOK FOUR: LOVE HIGH

Book Three: Big Time Love and Book Four: Love High Copyright 2016 by The Gemini Rising Rockin' Machine ISBN-13: 978-0692240939 (Gemini Rising Rockin' Machine,The) ISBN-10: 0692240934

All rights reserved. This book may not be reproduced, in whole or in part, without the written permission of the author, except for the purpose of reviews.

The characters and events described in this book are fictional. Any resemblance between the characters and any person including their names, living or dead, is purely coincidental.

Because of the mature themes presented within, reader discretion is advised.

For questions, comments you may send correspondence to.

thegeminirisingrockinmachine@twc.com.

Official Website
www.thegeminirisingrockinmachine.com

I Want To Be With You (493.) (New Cover Bonus)

Talking and Wanting as We-Look
Into-Each Other's-Eyes – Knowing
We're-Attached – Keeps-Us-Smiling
With a Deep-Down-Desire to Be-All-Alone

Time is Ticking-Away – We-Both-Know
We-Might Never-See – Each-Other-Again

(Chorus)
I Want To Be With You
You Look So Nice And Sweet
I Want To Be With You
Love Your Sexy Soft Voice
I Want To Be With You
Take You Away From A Silent Love
Straight Into An Love Explosion

Lonely-Eyes – Bodies-Shaking
We-Want to Fall in Love
Not-Say-Goodnight
Two-Hearts – Same-Idea
Here's-My-Number – Times-Two

(Chorus)
I Want To Be With You
You Look So Nice And Sweet
I Want To Be With You
Love Your Sexy Soft Voice
I Want To Be With You
Take You Away From A Silent Love
Straight Into An Love Explosion

Tasting and Feeling – We-Both
Fell in Love – While-Our-Clothes
Were-Lying – On the Floor
Two-Hearts – Same-Idea
Let-Them-Stay-There

(Repeat Chorus)

The Time Is Now (508.) (New Cover Bonus)

Oh-Baby – I-Need-You
You-Got-It – Going-On
Let-Me – Tell-Ya-Baby
I-Want-You so Sexy-Bad

If-You-Want a Man
That-Knows – How to Thrill
All – You – Gotta – Do
Is-Let – Your-Hair-Down
Let-Me – Turn-You-On

(Chorus)
The Time Is Now
Let's Go And Get It On
The Time Is Now
Let Your Lips Say Yes
Just Like Your Eyes Are Doing

Oh-Baby – Don't be Shy
You're so Hot and Fine
Grab-Your-Things-Baby
Follow – Come-With-Me

I'm-Taking-You – Home-Sweet-Home
So-You-Can – Get to Know
Me and My-Bed-Better – Baby

(Chorus)
The Time Is Now
Let's Go And Get It On
The Time Is Now
Let Your Lips Say Yes
Just Like Your Eyes Are Doing

Welcome – Come on In
Where – Magic – Happens
Every – Single – Sweet – Night
My-Place is the Place
Making-Love so Fine
Happens – All-The-Time

(Repeat Chorus)
3

Book Three: Big Time Love (Pages 4-35)
(The numbers after the song titles are the original numbering.)

(Side One)
41. Big Time Love (382.)
    Big Time Love (Is Pounding In My Heart) **(921.)**
42. It's So Nice To Be Loved (361.)
43. Little By Little (Duet) (323.)
44. Push Me Away (55.)
    You Came Back Broken (85 Days Later) **(914.)**
45. Our Love (40.)

(Side Two)
46. You Are My Everything (127.)
47. Somebody Loves Me (381.)
    Somebody Loves Me (In Mourning) **(915.)**
48. Catch My Heart (217.)
    Catch My Soul **(916.)**
49. Take My Hand (489.)
50. Ordinary (261.)

(Side Three)
51. Afraid Of Love (421.)
    I'm Not Afraid Of Love **(926.)**
52. Love (199.)
    I'm In Love **(924.)**
53. If You Need Me (563.)
54. Beautiful (142.)
55. A Beautiful Woman (420.)

(Side Four)
56. Fall In Love With Me (341.)
    Fall In Love With Me (Would Be Great) **(917.)**
57. One Day (The Hard / We Can Do It / Our Time Is Here) (250.)
58. Wrap My Love All Around You (394.)
59. Love Comes Back Around (561.)
60. The Lovers Of Forever (253.)

41. Big Time Love

One-Day – It-Just-Happens
Big-Time-Love – Collides-With-Your-Heart
You-Can-Run – You-Can-Hide
Or – You-Can-Grab – It-Up
Let-Love – Inside-Your-Heart

It's-Your-Choice – But-Remember
True-Love – Only-Comes-Around – Once
Here – Then-Gone-Forever
What-Are-You – Going to Do
Sing-This-Out-Loud – With-Me
Ready – 1-2-3 – Let's-Go

(Pre-Chorus)
Ain't No Love
Like Big Time Love
Making You Feel
So Big Time Loved
You're Full Of Desire – So Go Ahead
And Sing This Out Loud

(Chorus)
Big Time Love Is For Me
It Can Also Be For You
If You're Quick Enough
You Can Find Yourself – Some Special
Big Time Love – Just For You

You're-Doing-Great – Big-Time-Love
Has-Made-You – Shine so Bright
Don't-Get-That-Feeling – In-Your-Soul
It's-Okay – That-Was-Your-Yesterday

Everybody-Makes-Mistakes
Just-Smile – For the Day
Knowing – You're in Love
Will-Make-You – Want-To
Sing-This-Out-Loud – With-Me
Ready – 1-2-3 – Let's-Go

(Repeat Pre-Chorus & Chorus)

Big Time Love (Is Pounding In My Heart)

Hello-Morning-Sun
Thank-You for Your-Beauty
Great-News
I'm-All-Alone – No-More
That's-Right – Matter of Fact
I'm-Shining as Bright as You-Today

Out-My-Door – Here-I-Go
Hello-World – I'm in Love
How-You-Doing-Today
What-You-Say – You-Too
Well-Come-Over-Here
And-Sing-This – With-Me

(Chorus)
Big Time Love
Is Ticking In My Mind
Big Time Love
Is Pounding In My Heart
Big Time Love
Is Filling Up My Soul
Big Time Love – Big Time Love
Is The Greatest Thing On Earth

Hello-Nightly-Moon
You-Look so Very-Blue
It's-Your-Nature – I-Know
Still – Could-You – Shine a Little-Brighter
I'm-With-My-Love – This-Night
And-We-Feel – Like-Singing
Nightly-Moon – How-About-Singing-Along

(Chorus)
Big Time Love
Is Pounding In My Heart
Big Time Love
Is Ticking In My Mind
Big Time Love
Is Filling Up My Soul
Big Time Love – Big Time Love
Is The Greatest Thing On Earth

42. It's So Nice To Be Loved

It's so Very-Sad to Me – That-Everybody-Now-Seems
Not to Want-Love – They're so Down – Into-Their-Lives

It's-Just – Speeding-Away so Fast
When-They-Finally-Have – The-Time to Slow-Down
There's-No-One-Around – For-Them to Love

(Chorus)
It's So Nice To Be Loved
I Tell Ya
It's So Nice To Be Loved
You Know It
It's So Nice To Be Loved
Come On Everybody
It's So Nice To Be Loved

I-Don't-Have the Best-Life – A-Lot of Times
It's-One-Big-Old-Bummer – But-I-Never-Let-Life
Bring-Me-Down – Too-Far – Because – I-Have a Lot of Love
Inside-My-Heart – To-Keep-Me-Going-On

So-When-Life – Starts-To – Bring-Me-Down
I-Grab a Hold of My-Love – And-Give-Her a Great-Big-Kiss

(Chorus)
It's So Nice To Be Loved
I Tell Ya
It's So Nice To Be Loved
You Know It
It's So Nice To Be Loved
Come On Everybody
It's So Nice To Be Loved

If-You-Ever – Want to Know – How-Great-Love-Can-Be
Give-Me a Call – I'll-Let-You-Know

'Til-Then – Try-To – Do-Your-Best
To-Bring-Some-Love – Into-Your-Heart
Your-Life-Will-Be – So-Much-Better
Falling – And-Being – In-Love

(Repeat Chorus)

43. Little By Little (Duet)

(Her)
We're so New-Together
I-Don't-Even-Know – Your-Favorite-Color

(Him)
Taking-Our-Time is Kinda-Cool
But-My-Need – Is-Too-Great – To-Wait

(Her)
Our-Infatuations – Are-Blooming
It's-All-About-Passion – Right-Now
My-Wants – My-Needs – Are-Pulling-Me-Closer
Making-Me – Want to Lose-Control

(Him)
If-You-Ask-My-Heart
It-Would – Tell-You-This
I-Will-Fall – In-Love-With-You
The-Fist-Time – We-Make-Love

(Chorus)
(Together) Little by Little / **(Her)** Let's Take Our Time
(Together) Little by Little / **(Him)** Let's See What Happens
(Together) Little by Little / **(Her)** Maybe We'll Fall In Love
(Together) Little by Little / **(Together)** For The Rest Of Our Lives

(Her)
You're-What-I-Want – In a Man
Regretfully – I-Have-This-Feeling – That-You'll-Take
Then-Leave – Making-Me-Regret
That-I-Gave-You – What-You-Wanted
Instead of Waiting – 'Til-You-Loved-Me

(Chorus)
(Together) Little by Little / **(Her)** Let's Take Our Time
(Together) Little by Little / **(Him)** Let's See What Happens
(Together) Little by Little / **(Her)** Maybe We'll Fall In Love
(Together) Little by Little / **(Together)** For The Rest Of Our Lives

8

(Him)
Baby – Love is a Chance
I-Want-It – I-Think-I-Need-It
But-I-Can't-Wait – Much-Longer

I-Can't – Give-My-Heart to You
Until-I-Have a Taste – Of-Your-Flame
That-Way – I-Will-Know
Our-Love – Won't-Burn-Away

(Chorus)
(Together) Little by Little / **(Her)** Let's Take Our Time
(Together) Little by Little / **(Him)** Let's See What Happens
(Together) Little by Little / **(Her)** Maybe We'll Fall In Love
(Together) Little by Little / **(Together)** For The Rest Of Our Lives

(Her)
We're so New-Together
I-Don't-Even-Know – Your-Favorite-Color

(Him)
Taking-Our-Time is Kinda-Cool
But-My-Need – Is-Too-Great – To-Wait

(Her)
Our-Infatuations – Are-Blooming
It's-All-About-Passion – Right-Now

(Him)
I-Will-Fall – In-Love-With-You
The-Fist-Time – We-Make-Love

(Her)
You're-What-I-Want – In a Man

(Him)
Baby – Love is a Chance

(Chorus)
(Together) Little by Little / **(Her)** Let's Take Our Time
(Together) Little by Little / **(Him)** Let's See What Happens
(Together) Little by Little / **(Her)** Maybe We'll Fall In Love
(Together) Little by Little / **(Together)** For The Rest Of Our Lives

44. Push Me Away

I-Miss-You – So-Many-Moments
I-Feel-It – In-My-Heart
Rolling-Over – You're-Still-There
Your-Sweet-Scent
Almost-Lost to Me

(Chorus #1)
If You Have To / Push Me Away
To Have Your Space / To Feel Your Freedom
Push Me Away – Lover

We're a Memory – On the Edge – Of a Feather
Secrets-Forgotten – From-Past – Rainy-Days
Can-You-Remember – My-Heart
Our-Love – Has-Faded-Away

(Chorus #2)
Push Me Away / If You Have To
I'll Take It For Us / Push Me Away
Then Come Back / When You Love Me

I-Want to Hold – I Want to Kiss – You
Believe-My-Heart – That-Beats so True
Come-Back to Me – I'll-Never-Stop
I-Am-Not a Fool – To-Believe – In-Our-Love

(Chorus #1)
If You Have To / Push Me Away
To Have Your Space / To Feel Your Freedom
Push Me Away – Lover
(Repeat)

Love – Yes – Love – Is-What-I-Am
I'll-Be-Your – Everything
The-Laughs – The-Tears
I'll-Be-There – For-You

(Chorus #2)
Push Me Away / If You Have To
I'll Take It For Us / Push Me Away
Then Come Back / When You Love Me
(Repeat)

You Came Back Broken (85 Days Later)

85-Days-Later – You-Re-Enter-My-Life
Hug-Me so Tight
Tears – In-Your-Eyes
Happy – I'm-Still the Same

Love-Has-Not – Been-Kind
You-Sigh – So-Deeply
With-Wounds – On-Your-Body
Secrets – You-Can't-Keep
Made-You – Come-Back to Me

(Chorus)
Lover – You Are So Sad
You Came Back Broken
Lover – My Heart Is Frozen
You Came Back Broken
Lover – I Want To Feel Your Love
You Came Back Broken
Lover – I Wanted You To Love Me
You Came Back Broken
With No Love – In Your Heart

85-Days-Later – You-Re-Enter-My-Life
We're a Memory – On the Edge – Of a Feather
Secrets-Forgotten – From-Past – Rainy-Days
Our-Love – Has-Faded-Away

Love – What a Jester – Why-Was-I – Not-Enough
Love – I-Want-It – I-Can-Not-Stay
Our-Love – Has-Faded-Away – Becoming
A-Shattered-Rainbow – In a Gray – Empty-Sky

(Chorus)
Lover – You Are So Sad
You Came Back Broken
Lover – My Heart Is Frozen
You Came Back Broken
Lover – I Want To Feel Your Love
You Came Back Broken
Lover – I Wanted You To Love Me
You Came Back Broken
With No Love – In Your Heart

45. Our Love

Baby – I-Want-You-Back
It's-Been-Too-Long
Since-Our-Love – Was-Real
We – Were – Magic
Love – The-Power of Two

I-Let-Myself – Get-In the Way
Into-Our-Perfect-Love
Damn-Me – I-Am-Weak – So-Weak

I-Let-Myself – Stray
Letting-You-Fall – Out of My-Mind
So-I-Could – Have a Moment – With-Another-Lover

(Chorus)
Baby – Oh Baby
Don't Know Why
I Did This To Us
Please Forgive Me
Take Me Back – 'Cause It's
The Right Thing – For Our Love

Baby – I-Want-You-Back
Even-Though – I-Done-You – So-Wrong
Our-Love – Is-Worth the Sacrifice
Baby – Give-Me – One-More-Chance
I'll-Make-It – Up to You
That's-It-Baby – Take-Me-Back

We-Are the Two – That is One – Once-Again
I-Love-You – You-Love-Me
Our-Love is So-Strong
That-Deep-Down – Desire-I-Feel
Is-Now – Only-For-You – I-Promise

(Chorus)
Baby – Oh Baby
Don't Know Why
I Did This To Us
Please Forgive Me
Take Me Back – 'Cause It's
The Right Thing – For Our Love

46. You Are My Everything

Alone – For so Long
Never-Feeling a True-Connection
Love-Was-Everywhere
But it Never – Found-Me

My-Heart – Almost-Turned to Stone
Then-You – Found-Me
Came-Right-Up - and - Said-Hello
Your-Eyes – Were-From-Heaven
That-Penetrated – My-Soul

(Chorus)
I'm Going To Keep
Loving You Baby
No Matter What
'Cause Baby I Know
You Are My Everything
My Everything – That I Love

I-Had-Nothing – Loneliness
Loveless – Cold and Wanting
Fake-Smiling-Myself – Through-Life
Putting-Myself – Out-There
Trying to Join-In – On-Life

Then – The-Storm-Stopped
Not a Cloud – In the Sky
Wonderment – Befell-Me
As-Sunshine – Entered-My-Heart

I'm-Not-Broken – Anymore
I-Love the Day – I-Love-Life
No-More-Skips – No-More-Stops
Only-Love – Inside-My-Heart

(Chorus)
I'm Going To Keep
Loving You Baby
No Matter What
'Cause Baby I Know
You Are My Everything
My Everything – That I Love
13

47. Somebody Loves Me

I-Lose-Myself – In-Your-Eyes
You're the Calm
Of-My – Long-Day
I-Love-You-Baby
Give-Me a Hug – Give-Me a Kiss

I'm so Happy – Being in Love
Yesterday – Was-Sad and Lonely
Today – Is a Day – That-Makes-Me
Feel-Good – About-Being-Alive

(Chorus)
Somebody Loves Me
I'm Not Alone
After So Long
Of Being This way
Finally Out Of Nowhere
Somebody Loves Me
Ain't That A Kick To The Heart

I-Know – I'm-Falling-Fast
For-You – I-Can't-Help-It
This is Big-Time-Love
I-Never-Felt – Before

I'm-Going to Try
To-Take-It a Little-Easy
So-I-Don't – Screw-It-Up
Smother-Away
My-Big-Time-Love
That-Finally – Found its Way
Into-My-Heart

(Chorus)
Somebody Loves Me
I'm Not Alone
After So Long
Of Being This way
Finally Out Of Nowhere
Somebody Loves Me
Ain't That A Kick To The Heart

Somebody Loves Me (In Mourning)

We-Were-Happy – You-We're-Alive
We-Were in Love – You-We're-Not-Dead
Everyday – I-Loved-My-Wife
Everyday – I-Loved-My-Life
Bang-Bang – You-Died
In-My-Arms – Crying and Bleeding
While a Monster – Ran-Away

No-Love – In-My-Heart
I-Left-Everything – Behind
I-Hate-My-Life – I-Hate this World
My-Soul is So-Cold
I-Wish – That-Bullet – Found-Me
Instead of My-Love

(Chorus)
Somebody Loves Me
I'm Not Alone
After So Long
Of Being In Mourning
Finally Out Of Nowhere
Somebody Loves Me
Ain't That A Kick – Twice To The Heart

God in Heaven – Why-Her
Devil in Hell – She's an Angel
Far and Free – From-Your-Touch
I-Love-This – This-Makes-Me-Cry

Damn it All – I'm-All-Alone – Without-My-Friend
What's the Point – In-Living
Without-My-Wife – In-My-Life
God in Heaven – Devil in Hell
I-Want-My-Wife – Back-Alive

My-Heart – Has-Turned to Stone
Then-You – Found-Me
Came-Right-Up - and - Said-Hello
Your-Eyes – Were-From-Heaven
That-Penetrated – My-Soul

(Repeat Chorus)
15

48. Catch My Heart

I-Have-Seen-You – Many-Times
You're-That – Pretty-Lady
That-I-Look-Forward to Seeing
Everyday – At the Same-Time

While-Waiting for Our – Morning-Coffee
I-Know by Heart – How-You-Like-Yours
You're a Lover of Habit
Just-Like – I-Am

(Chorus)
Catch My Heart
I Know That I'm Not
What You Had In Mind
But All You Gotta Do Is
Hold Out Your Hands
Catch My Heart
And It Will Belong To You
For As Long – As You Want To Love It

I-Always – Tell-Myself
That-Today – Is the Day
I-Say – No-More-Waiting

The-Day – I-Finally – Say-Hello
Can-I-Buy-You – Your-Coffee
I'd-Like to Fall in Love-Today
But-First-Please – Can-You
Tell-Me-Your-Name

(Chorus)
Catch My Heart
I Know That I'm Not
What You Had In Mind
But All You Gotta Do Is
Hold Out Your Hands
Catch My Heart
And It Will Belong To You
For As Long – As You Want To Love It

Catch My Soul

Been-There – Done-That
Love-Was a Friend to My-Heart
Even-Though-Sometimes
Love-Gave-Me – A-Heart-Ache

As-I-Sit – In-This-Jet
That is On-Fire and Going-Down
I-Remember a Great-Day
The-Beach – A-Hot-Lady – With-Me
That's-Built – For a Two-Piece

(Chorus)
Well God – Looks Like I'm Dying
Thanks For The Crashing Death
I Really Loved My Life
I'm Not Ready To Die
So God – The Least You Can Do Is
Catch My Soul – Before It Lands In Hell

Hey God – How About Doing Me A Solid
You-Have-Nothing – But-Time
I'm-Sitting-Here – The-Seat-Behind-Me – Is-On-Fire
Is-This-My-Omen – Am-I-Damned

Wow-God – Give a Man a Break
I'm-Not-That-Big of a Sinner
So-I-Lusted – Many-Times – Who-Hasn't
I'm-Not-Perfect – But-I'm-Built for Heaven

Look at Your-Great-Work in Action
Have a Heart – Give-Me-Heaven
You-Know-I – Don't-Deserve to Be in Hell
By the Way-God – Did-I-Mention – That-I-Love-You

(Chorus)
Well God – Looks Like I'm Dying
Thanks For The Crashing Death
I Really Loved My Life
I'm Not Ready To Die
So God – The Least You Can Do Is
Catch My Soul – Before It Lands In Hell

49. Take My Hand

Come on Baby – Grab-Your-Bags
Let's-Get – Out of Here
Before-Our-Lives – Turn into Dust
I-Want to See – Something-New
With-You by My-Side
Hand in Hand – Still in Love

We're-Use to Bumps
Things-Going-Wrong
Like-Being-Trapped – In a Home
That is Falling-Apart

(Chorus)
You're The Love Of My Life
I Love You So Much
All I Ask Of You – My Love
Is For You – To Take My Hand
As I Lead Us – To Our Freedom

Our-Road is Filled-Up
With-Such – Wonderful-Sights
As-We-Stop and Stay-Awhile
Getting to Know – Some-Good-People
Our-Road is Also – Filled-With-Places
That-Just-Don't – Feel-Right
So-We-Avoid the Bad-Bumps
And-Just-Keep-On – Riding-Along

When-Mother-Nature's-Fury
Brings-Down the Hard-Rains
Soaking-Us – To-Our-Bones
We'll-Stop-Riding – We'll-Weather the Storm
Then-We'll – Ride-On – When the Sun – Shines-Down
Warming-Our-Bodies – To-Match-Our-Love

(Chorus)
You're The Love Of My Life
I Love You So Much
All I Ask Of You – My Love
Is For You – To Take My Hand
As I Lead Us – To Our Freedom

18

50. Ordinary

Rose is a Waitress – At a Top-Less-Bar
She's as Pretty – As-Her-Name
That-Brightens – This-Dark-Place-Up

Rose-Dances to Your-Table – Top-Less
You-Can-Look – All-You-Want
Just-Don't-Touch or You'll-Get a Smack

Silly-Rose – Never-Wants to Have-Any-Fun
But in My-Mind – She's-Full of Desire
I-Wish-Just-Once – She-Would-Say-Yes

(Chorus)
Rose Might Think She's Ordinary
Not Giving It Much Thought
Even Though Men are Always Asking
Rose Just Smiles And Says No
She'd Rather Be By Herself
For Alone Is Comfortable
It's Rose's Ordinary

Another-End of a Night – I'm-Broke
Gave-All-My-Money to Rose
But-Damn – Do-I-Have a Buzz

Walking – Trying to Walk
Wow – Could-I-Use – Some-Loving
Pretty-Rose – Would be Perfect

There-She is Now – With-Tears in Her-Eyes
Here's-My-Chance – What-Do-I-Have to Lose
Hey-Pretty-Rose – Would-You-Like-Me – To-Pluck-You

(Chorus)
Rose Might Think She's Ordinary
Not Giving It Much Thought
Even Though Men are Always Asking
Rose Just Smiles And Says No
She'd Rather Be By Herself
For Alone Is Comfortable
It's Rose's Ordinary

51. Afraid Of Love

I-Tell-You – This-My-Friend
Because-You're too Stubborn
To-See-This for Yourself
Love is Beautiful – Love is Blind
Love-Can-Last for Years
Or it Can-Last – Only for Days

Most-Love – Has a Shelf-Life
Then-There's – That-One-Love
That-Makes-You-Feel-It
You-Have to Go – Through a Lot
Before-You – Catch-Up
With the Love of Your-Life

(Chorus)
You Can Do Anything
You Can Run – You Can Hide
You Can Kick – You Can Scream
But You Can't Be – Afraid Of Love
Because-One-Day – It Will Find You

I-Tell-You – This-My-Friend
Because-You're too Stubborn
To-See-This for Yourself
Love is Beautiful – Love is Blind
Love-Can-Last for Years
Or it Can-Last – Only for Days

Most-Love – Has a Shelf-Life
Then-There's – That-One-Love
That-Makes-You-Feel-It
You-Have to Go – Through a Lot
Before-You – Catch-Up
With the Love of Your-Life

(Chorus)
You Can Do Anything
You Can Run – You Can Hide
You Can Kick – You Can Scream
But You Can't Be – Afraid Of Love
Because-One-Day – It Will Find You

I'm Not Afraid Of Love

The-Sky is Dark
The-World is Wild
I'm-Not-Afraid of Love
Lovers-Come – Mine-Left-Yesterday
I'm Heartbroken – Still
I'm-Not-Afraid of Love

Driving-Down the Road – My-Car-Stops
I'm 300 Miles – Away-From-Home
I'm-Not-Afraid of Love
I've-Stepped in a Puddle
I-Have a Hole in My-Shoe
Still – I'm-Not-Afraid of Love

(Chorus)
One Day – I'll Be Doing Fine
One Day – I'll Have More Than
Twenty Dollars In My Pocket
One Day – But Not Today
That's Okay – That's Fine – Because
I'm-Not-Afraid Of Love
No-No-No – I'm-Not-Afraid Of Love
So Come On Love – Come And Get Me

The-Sky- is Dark
The-World is Wild
I'm-Not-Afraid of Love
Lovers-Come – Mine-Left-Yesterday
I'm Heartbroken – Still
I'm-Not-Afraid of Love
And-Why-Should-I-Be
I'm-Loveable and So-Is-My-Love

(Chorus)
One Day – I'll Be Doing Fine
One Day – I'll Have More Than
Twenty Dollars In My Pocket
One Day – But Not Today
That's Okay – That's Fine – Because
I'm-Not-Afraid Of Love
No-No-No – I'm-Not-Afraid Of Love
So Come On Love – Come And Get Me

52. Love

Love is Happiness
Happiness is Love
Love is Sadness
Sadness is Love

Love is Togetherness
Togetherness is Love
Love is Loneliness
Loneliness is Love

Love is Everything
And-Everything is Love
Come-On-World – Repeat-This-With-Me

(Chorus)
Love – Is What We Have
Love – Is Our Way Of Life
Love – Keeps Us Strong
Love – Keeps Us True
Love – Will Save The World

Love is Happiness
Happiness is Love
Love is Sadness
Sadness is Love

Love is Togetherness
Togetherness is Love
Love is Loneliness
Loneliness is Love

Love is Everything
And-Everything is Love
Come-On-World – Repeat-This-With-Me

(Chorus)
Love – Is What We Have
Love – Is Our Way Of Life
Love – Keeps Us Strong
Love – Keeps Us True
Love – Will Save The World

I'm In Love

No-Love – Last-Year
No-Love – Last-Month
No-Love-Yesterday
However-Today – I'm-In-Love

Just-Like-That – I'm-In-Love
Pretty-Lady – Kissed-My-Lips
Pretty-Lady – Kissed-My-Heart
Now-Today – I'm-In-Love

What a Day – Can't-Wait-To-See
What-She-Has in Store – For-Me-Tonight

(Chorus)
I'm-In-Love – Can't You See
I'm-In-Love – Can't You Tell
I'm-In-Love – Hooray For Me
I'm-In-Love – World
It Feels So Good To Be In Love
I Wish You Could Feel It Too

No-Love – Last-Year
No-Love – Last-Month
No-Love-Yesterday
However-Today – I'm-In-Love

Just-Like-That – I'm-In-Love
Pretty-Lady – Kissed-My-Lips
Pretty-Lady – Kissed-My-Heart
Now-Today – I'm-In-Love

What a Day – Can't-Wait-To-See
What-She-Has in Store – For-Me-Tonight

(Chorus)
I'm-In-Love – Can't You See
I'm-In-Love – Can't You Tell
I'm-In-Love – Hooray For Me
I'm-In-Love – World
It Feels So Good To Be In Love
I Wish You Could Feel It Too

53. If You Need Me

Love is All-Powerful
Love is Alive and Blooming
Everywhere – Around the World
But-You-Got-To – Watch-Love

Because-It – Can-Rip
Your – Heart – Out
Paralyze – Your-Soul
Even-Control-You
If-You-Let-It

(Chorus)
If You Need Me
I'm Right Here
Just Come On Over
If You Need Me
I'd Love To Help You
Fall In Love Again

Sex and Fantasy are Great
Helps – You – Cope
When-You're-Having a Great-Time
When-You're-Looking for Love

Sex – Can-Be the Answer
To a Long-Time of Loneliness
Just-Don't-Forget
To-Walk-Away – Before-You
Confuse-It – For-Love

(Chorus)
If You Need Me
I'm Right Here
Just Come On Over
If You Need Me
I'd Love To Help You
Fall In Love Again

(Come on Everybody)

If-You-Need-Me
I'll-Be-Here to Give-You a Hand
If-You-Need-Me
I'll-Be-Here to Give-You a Hug
If-You-Need-Me
I'll-Be-Here to Give-You a Kiss

If-You-Need-Me
I'll-Be-Here to Give-You – Some-Lovin'
If-You-Need-Me
I'll-Be-Glad to Make-Love to You
If-You-Need-Me
I'll-Be-Glad to Come-Back – Over-Tomorrow

(Chorus)
If You Need Me
I'm Right Here
Just Come On Over
If You Need Me
I'd Love To Help You
Fall In Love Again

(Come On Everybody)

If-You-Need-Me
I'll-Be-Here to Give-You a Hand
If-You-Need-Me
I'll-Be-Here to Give-You a Hug
If-You-Need-Me
I'll-Be-Here to Give-You a Kiss

If-You-Need-Me
I'll-Be-Here to Give-You – Some-Lovin'
If-You-Need-Me
I'll-Be-Glad to Make-Love to You
If-You-Need-Me
I'll-Be-Glad to Come-Back – Over-Tomorrow

(Repeat Chorus)

54. Beautiful

We-Got-Together
Having a Great-Time
You're so Beautiful
Makes-Me – Not-Care
Why-You're-With-Me
As-Long as You-Stay
And-Never – Fly-Away

(Pre-Chorus)
Together-We-Make – The-Hot-Couple
That-Every-Couple – Wants to Be
Having a Great-Time – Out and About
Even a Better-Time – When-We-Get-Home

(Chorus)
Beautiful
My Lady Is Beautiful
Beautiful
Just Looking At Her
Beautiful
I-Get to Make-Sweet-Love – To-My-Beautiful-Love

We-Are-Human – We-Have-Our-Temptations
They-Are-Out-There – In-Waiting
We-Look – But-Never-Touch
I'm-Glad – You're-Glad
That-We-Are – Staying-In-Love

(Pre-Chorus)
Together-We-Make – The-Hot-Couple
That-Every-Couple – Wants to Be
Having a Great-Time – Out and About
Even a Better-Time – When-We-Get-Home

(Chorus)
Beautiful
My Lady Is Beautiful
Beautiful
Just Looking At Her
Beautiful
I-Get to Make-Sweet-Love – To-My-Beautiful-Love

55. A Beautiful Woman

Looks-Are so Important
It's-What – Turns-Us-On
That-Moment of Hot-Passion
That-Turns-Gray – Into-Blue

We-All-Want-Love
But it Comes-Around so Slow
Making-Us – Not-Pay-Attention
To the Chance – That-We-Just-Lost
While-Coasting-By – Without-Even-Noticing-It
And-I'm-Tired of Playing it Slow

(Chorus)
A Beautiful Woman
Is a Beautiful Woman
If You're Lucky Enough
To Have One Enter Your Life
You Have To Give Her – A Honest Love
Not A Love – That Will Smother Her

You're so Lonely – Without-Love
She's-Looking at You – With-That-Smile
You've-Seen so Many-Times
But-This-Time – It-Seems-Different
The-Girl – Next-Door to You
Who's-Always-Only – Been-Your-Friend

She's-Not a Model – She's a Beautiful-Woman
That-You – Get-Along-With
She's-Seen-You-Sick – She's-Seen-You-Ugly
She-Smells so Nice – She-Looks so Pretty
With a Figure – You-Notice
That-Looks – Twice as Nice
Makes-You-Want to Be – More-Than-Friends

(Chorus)
A Beautiful Woman
Is a Beautiful Woman
If You're Lucky Enough
To Have One Enter Your Life
You Have To Give Her – A Honest Love
Not A Love – That Will Smother Her

56. Fall In Love With Me

Loneliness is So-Lonely
It-Crept-Up – On-Me
Before-I-Noticed-It
It-Found its Way
Straight-Through – My-Heart
Making-It so Hard – On-Me
To-Feel-Love – Inside-My-Heart

(Chorus)
Hello Out There
I'm All Alone – Without-Love
I Was Just Wondering
If Anybody Out There
Knows Somebody That Wants To
Fall In Love With Me

Life's so Funny
Where-Were – All-These-Ladies
When-I-Wasn't – Looking for Love
When-I-Was-Just-Out – To-Have a Night-Full
Of-Good-Good – Sweet-Lovin'

A-Good-Time or Ten – Has-Been-Great
Just-What-I – Truly-Needed
But it's Time to Think of My-Heart
That's-Beating – Fast and True
Making-Me-Ready
To-Find-Some – True-Fine-Love
That-My-Loveless-Soul – Needs to Feel so Bad

(Chorus)
Hello Out There
I'm All Alone – Without-Love
I Was Just Wondering
If Anybody Out There
Knows Somebody That Wants To
Fall In Love With Me

Fall In Love With Me (Would Be Great)

I'm-Alone – You're-Alone
I-Like-Your-Dress
Are-You-Waiting on a Date
I-Understand – Lucky-Guy

I'm-Alone – You're-Alone
I-Like-Your – Short-Skirt
Would-You – Like to Make-Out
Would-You – Like to Make-Love
I-Understand – Just-Sex – Would be Great

(Chorus)
Hello Out There
I'm All Alone – Without-Love
I Was Just Wondering
If Anybody Out There
Knows Somebody That Wants To
Fall In Love With Me

I'm-Alone – You're-Alone
I-Like-Your-Dress
Would-You-Like to Take a Walk
Would-You-Like to Talk
I-Understand – Lucky-Guy

I'm-Alone – You're-Alone
I-Like-Your – Short-Skirt
Would-You-Like to Have-Dinner-First
How-About-Dessert
I-Understand – Just-Sex – Would be Great

(Chorus)
Hello Out There
I'm All Alone – Without-Love
I Was Just Wondering
If Anybody Out There
Knows Somebody That Wants To
Fall In Love With Me

57. One Day (The Hard / We Can Do It / Our Time Is Here)

(The Hard)

We-Fell in Love
Took-Our-Time
Before-Getting-Married
We-Stayed in Love
Then – One – Day
The-Hard-On-Us
Was so Hard
That-We-Felt-It
All the Way to Our-Souls

Everyday – Was the Same
And it Was the Same-Everyday
The-Hard – Never-Went-Away
It-Set-Up-Shop
Just to Torment-Us
We-Stayed-Strong
We-Stayed in Love

(Chorus)
One Day – The Hard Was Not So Hard
One Day – It Got Easier For us
One Day – We Started To Smile
One Day – We Made Love And Laughed
One Day – Our Lives Became A Lot Better

(We Can Do It)

Ready-Now-Baby
Let's-Get-Started
We-Can-Do-It
Baby-We-Can-Do-It
We've-Got to Get-Going
Before it's Too-Late
We-Can-Do-It
Baby-We-Can-Do-It

Our-Time is Getting-Closer
We-Worked so Hard for This
We-Can-Do-It
Baby-We-Can-Do-It
It's-Our-Chance
To-Take a Bite – Out of Life
That's-Been – Denied to Us
We-Can-Do-It
Baby-We-Can-Do-It

(Chorus)
One Day – The Hard Was Not So Hard
One Day – It Got Easier For us
One Day – We Started To Smile
One Day – We Made Love And Laughed
One Day – Our Lives Became A Lot Better

(Our Time Is Here)

It-Took – Half of Our-Lives
This-Means – Nothing-Now
Knowing-We – Have-Our-Love
And the Stars to Play-With
Our-Time is Here
Baby-Our – Time Is Here

We-Look at Each-Other
Both of Us – Knowing-It to Be for Real
Because-Our – Loving-Eyes – Says it's So
Our-Time is Here
Baby-Our – Time Is Here

(Chorus)
One Day – The Hard Was Not So Hard
One Day – It Got Easier For us
One Day – We Started To Smile
One Day – We Made Love And Laughed
One Day – Our Lives Became A Lot Better

58. Wrap My Love All Around You

If-You-Need-Me
I'm-All-Alone
Reach-Out and Grab-Me
I'll-Be-So-Glad-To
Wrap-My-Love – Around-You

Trust – Me – Darling
I'll be Your-Friend
And as Lovers
We'll-Ascend to The-Stars
We're-Special – We're in Love
And-Baby – All-I-Have to Say – Is

(Chorus)
Come To Me Darling
If You Need Some Lovin'
I'm Right Here – Ready To Be Your One
All You Have To Do Is – Let Yourself Go
As I – Wrap My Love – All-Around You

If-You-Need-Me
I'm-All-Alone
Reach-Out and Grab-Me
I'll-Be-So-Glad-To
Wrap-My-Love – Around-You

Trust – Me – Darling
I'll be Your-Friend
And as Lovers
We'll-Ascend to The-Stars
We're-Special – We're in Love
And-Baby – All-I-Have to Say – Is

(Chorus)
Come To Me Darling
If You Need Some Lovin'
I'm Right Here – Ready To Be Your One
All You Have To Do Is – Let Yourself Go
As I – Wrap My Love – All-Around You

59. Love Comes Back Around

She was My – First-Love
She-Really-Rocked – My-World
All-Summer – We-Were-In the
Height of Passion – Only to Drift-Away
Like-Falling-Leaves – When the Winds of Change
Came-Blowing-In – Chilling-Our-Hearts

(Chorus)
Love Comes Back Around
When You're Smiling – When You're Crying
Love Comes Back Around
When You're Not Even – Looking For It
Love Comes Back Around
Even When You're – Already In Love
Love Comes Back Around – Oh Yes It Does

Met-Her – On a Friday – We-Were in Love by
Saturday-Morning-Breakfast
Tomorrow-Didn't-Matter – Neither-Did-Next-Week
Then-One-Day – She-Went-Away – Almost-Breaking
My-Heart – Leaving-Me-All-Alone – Without-Love
But-I-Kept the Faith – Because...

(Chorus)
Love Comes Back Around
When You're Smiling – When You're Crying
Love Comes Back Around
When You're Not Even – Looking For It
Love Comes Back Around
Even When You're – Already In Love
Love Comes Back Around – Oh Yes It Does

Love is Alive in The-World
She-Spilled a Drink on Me
Didn't-Matter – As-I-Looked into Her-Eyes
Love is Alive in The-World
As-She-Said – I-Do – A-Few-Years-Later
Proving to Me – What-I've-Already-Known
That – Love is Alive in The-World

(Repeat Chorus)

33

60. The Lovers Of Forever

Love is a Treat – Love is a Trick
I'm an Old-Soul – That's-In-Love
Fourth-Time's the Charm
She's to Be – My-Wife
Wasn't-Looking-For a Fifth
Until-I-Looked into Her-Eyes

Pure-Bliss – Inside-My-Heart
We-Stand-Still – Remembering the Other
Years – So-Many-Years – Have-Gone-By
We-Touch-Hands – We're-One-Again

(Chorus)
I Love Her
I Know I Shouldn't
I Belong To Another
I Can't Help Myself
For We Are The Lovers Of Forever
And We Just Found Each Other Again

I'm-Sorry-My-Love – Sorry-I-Broke-Your-Heart
I-Love-You – You'll-Never-Understand
I-Cannot-Help-Myself – I-Have to Leave-You
She is My-Forever-Love
I'm-Her-King – She's-My-Queen

Please-Don't-Cry – You-Can't-Fight-Fate
My-Love and I – We-Are the Moon
We-Are the Sun – We-Are the Stars
Heaven-Has – Blessed-Us
We-Are-The – Lovers of Forever
Goodbye – My-Former – Love of My-Life

(Chorus)
I Love Her
I Know I Shouldn't
I Belong To Another
I Can't Help Myself
For We Are The Lovers Of Forever
And We Just Found Each Other Again

Dear Love,
I Miss You. I Miss You so Much.
Everyday seems like an Eternity
Since we've been Apart.
Very soon my Darling
I will be Making my way Home to You.
I can't Wait to See your Smile.

Dear Love,
I am Sorry I Broke your Heart,
But what Could I do?
I had to Pay you Back
For Breaking my Heart in the First place.
Now that we are Even
Stop Complaining & Come Over
So we can Have some more Fun.

Dear Love,
I have great News for You my Love!
It Happened!
What we've been Waiting for,
My big Break is Finally here.
So put on Your – Prettiest Dress
I'll pick you up & we'll Hit the Town.

Dear Love,
I told You I Loved you.
I told You I was Sorry.
I told You – You were Wrong,
But You still will not Believe me.
So after all these Years together
I'm Sad to Say to You -
Good Bye, You blew it Baby.

35

Break Me When You're Done With Me (28.) (Bonus Reprint)

Time and Time – I-Have-Tried
To-Find that Special-Person
That-Wants to Give – Me-Their-Love
And-Take-Mine in Return
I-Have-Tried so Hard
Being-Someone – I-Think-They-Want
Erasing-What – Makes-Me – Me
And-All-They-Do – Is-Use – Then-Break-Me

(Chorus)
I Guess I Forgot To Remove
My Tag That Reads
Break Me When You're Done With Me
I Wish I Would Remember
This Seems To Happen Every Time
And I Am Tired Of Being Broken

Set-Ups – Blind-Dates – Chance-Meetings
I-Have-Done-Them-All – Many-Times
Seems-Great – For-Only a Good-Time
Because-Soon – They-Are-Gone
When-They-Get-Restless – Or-Tired of Me
I am Alone – Once-Again – Wondering-Why
What-Did-I – Or – Didn't-I-Do – This-Time

(Chorus)
I Guess I Forgot To Remove
My Tag That Reads
Break Me When You're Done With Me
I Wish I Would Remember
This Seems To Happen Every Time
And I Am Tired Of Being Broken

Why – Please-Tell-Me-Why
I'm a Good-Person – Keep-Myself-Clean
Have a Lot of Love to Give-Away
Why am I – Not-Good-Enough to be Loved-Forever
Please-Somebody – Come to Me – I've-Fallen – Pick-Me-Up
I-Do-Not-Want – My-Heart to Turn to Stone
And for My-Love to Dry-Up and Become-Decayed

(Repeat Chorus)
36

All I Need (06.) (Bonus Reprint)

This-Lonely-Night – Begs for Love
The-Love – Only-You-Have – For-Me
All-These-Long-Nights – Without-You
It's-All-I-Can-Do – Not to Lose-Control
It's-All-I-Can-Do – Not to Explode

We're-Going to Be-Together
Finally – To-Touch-You-Again
I-Have-Missed-You – Oh so Much

(Chorus)
'Cause Baby You're All I Need
To Make Me Feel So Right
I Can Go Through Anything
There's Nothing That I Won't Do
'Cause Baby You're All I Need

Let's-Forget – All-That-Bad
Get-Back to Some-Good
You-Know – As-well as I
That-We're-Better – With-Each-Other

Nothing-Wrong – With-That
It's-Great as Matter of Fact
So-Many – Have-Nothing – Just-Loneliness
They-Will-Never-Know – What-We-Have

(Chorus)
'Cause Baby You're All I Need
To Make Me Feel So Right
I Can Go Through Anything
There's Nothing That I Won't Do
'Cause Baby You're All I Need

(Chorus)
'Cause Baby You're All I Need
To Make Me Feel So Right
I Can Go Through Anything
There's Nothing That I Won't Do
'Cause Baby You're All I Need

Book Four: Love High (Pages 38-70)
(The numbers after the song titles are the original numbering)

(Side One)
61. Love High (536.)
    Get High On Love **(920.)**
62. She's Got To Be Mine (132.)
63. Love Baby Love (43.)
64. Time (238.)
65. Stay (239.)
    Stay (What's The Point) **(918.)**

(Side Two)
66. High With Me (327.)
67. (I'm Busted) For I've Fallen In Love With You (457.)
68. Sweet Sweet Love (66.)
    Sweet Love (That Sticks Around) **(922.)**
69. Pillow Talk (207.)
    Pillow Talk (I'm A Pillow Talker) **(923.)**
70. Summer Time And Love (540.)
    Summer Time And Love (What A Great Mixture) **(919.)**

(Side Three)
71. Happy Birthday Baby (422.)
    I Only Dream Of You (868) **(Bonus Song)**
72. She Let Me Pick Her (97.)
73. Smile If You Love Me (578.)
74. Makes Me Smile (502.)
75. It's Time For Love (451.)

(Side Four)
(Sex With No Love: 76-77)
76. Let's Be Friends (That Sleep Together) (319.)
77. Forget About Our Love (320.)
78. Turn Me On Baby (522.)
    Let Me Turn You On **(925.)**
79. She Still Has That Body (558.)
    Sexy Bodies (Look At That Sexy Body) **(927.)**
80. Lady From Space (Love Version) (346.)

61. Love High

You-Floated – In-My-Direction
Giving-Me – Such a Love-High
You-Re-Woke – My-Life
My-Mind – Body and Soul
Was in Love-High – Heaven

(Chorus)
Your Love High / Is So Intoxicating
I've Become Addicted / To Your Super Love High
Your Love High / Is So Intoxicating
I've Become Addicted / To Your Super Love High
Your Love High / Is So Intoxicating
I Never Want To Come Down

The-Smile on Your-Lips
The-Shake of Your-Hips
Brings-Me – Such-Delight
I-Want to Overdose – On the Heavenly
Love-High – You-Keep-Giving-Me
Every – Single – Sweet – Night

(Chorus)
Your Love High / Is So Intoxicating
I've Become Addicted / To Your Super Love High
Your Love High / Is So Intoxicating
I've Become Addicted / To Your Super Love High
Your Love High / Is So Intoxicating
I Never Want To Come Down

In the Dark – When-We're-Hot
When – We're – Getting-It-On
You-Tell-Me – Not to Think
Just-Enjoy – Your-Love-High
As-You-Consume-Me – Even-More
I'm-Not-Myself – Anymore
I'm-Just-Your-Man
And-I-Don't – Love-High-Mind
One-Little – Love-High-Bit

(Repeat Chorus)

Get High On Love

I-Was in Love – She-Cheated on Me
I-Fell in Love-Again
She-Cheated on Me-Too
I-Fell in Love – Once-Again
She-Cheated on Me – With-My-Best-Friend

Boo to You-World – Boo to You-Love
I'm a Great-Lover – I-Deserve-Better
I'm so Down – What-Can-I-Do
To-Get-Myself – Out of This – Love-Funk

(Chorus)
I'm Going To – I'm Going To
Get High On Love
That's What I'm Going to Do
Love You World – What's Your Problem
If You Won't Help Me
I'm Going To – I'm Going To
Get High On Love
All By Myself – Without You

I-Was in Love – She-Cheated on Me
I-Fell in Love-Again
She-Cheated on Me-Too
I-Fell in Love – Once-Again
She-Cheated on Me – With-My-Best-Friend

Boo to You-World – Boo to You-Love
I'm a Great-Lover – I-Deserve-Better
I'm so Down – What-Can-I-Do
To-Get-Myself – Out of This – Love-Funk

(Chorus)
I'm Going To – I'm Going To
Get High On Love
That's What I'm Going to Do
Love You World – What's Your Problem
If You Won't Help Me
I'm Going To – I'm Going To
Get High On Love
All By Myself – Without You

62. She's Got To Be Mine

Here-Comes a Heart-Attack
In-Tight-Pants and a See-Thru-Top

The-Best-Part of Me – Is-Already-Saying-Hello
Please-Baby-Please – Don't be Cruel
Give-It-To-Me – Give-It-To-Me-Please

Hello-Lady – That is So-Fine
Excuse-My-Bulge – Excuse-My-Drooling
Would-You-Like to Come-Home-With-Me

(Chorus)
She's Got To Be Mine
Just Look At Her
She's So Sweet – She's So Fine
She's Got To Be Mine
I Want To Love Her
For A Very Long Time

Here's-My-Place
Make-Yourself at Home – Relax
Take-Off-Your-Shoes – Have a Drink

My-Bedroom is the Second-Door on The-Right
Please-Take-Off-Your-Clothes
When-You-Feel-Like – Making-Love

Yes-I-Move-Fast – Just-Like-My-Heart
Beats for You – Waiting is for Yesterday
While-Tomorrow – We'll-Still-Be-In-Bed
Making-Love as Loving-Lovers

(Chorus)
She's Got To Be Mine
Just Look At Her
She's So Sweet – She's So Fine
She's Got To Be Mine
I Want To Love Her
For A Very Long Time

63. Love Baby Love

Hello-Baby – It's-Me
I-Thought-I'd-Try – One-More-Time
To-Let-You-Know – That-I'm the Real-Thing

Please-Notice-Me – Give-Me-One-Chance
I'll-Be so Good to You – You'll-Never
Have to Look – For-Love – Ever- Again

(Chorus)
Love Baby Love
That's What I Have For You
Love Baby Love
You Need It – I Can Tell
Love Baby Love
Give Into It – It Will Never Fade Away
Love Baby Love
You Can Look Everywhere
And Never Find One So True
Love Baby Love
That's What I Have For You

This-Time it's Love – Comin' for You
Not a One-Time – Or – 'Til-I'm-Bored
I-Look at You – I-Feel – Weak-All-Over

Please—Notice-Me – Give-Me-One-Chance
I'll-Be so Good to You – You'll-Never
Have to Look – For-Love – Ever- Again

(Chorus)
Love Baby Love
That's What I Have For You
Love Baby Love
You Need It – I Can Tell
Love Baby Love
Give Into It – It Will Never Fade Away
Love Baby Love
You Can Look Everywhere
And Never Find One So True
Love Baby Love
That's What I Have For You

64. Time

We-Were-Young – We-Fell in Love
Time-Took-Our-Love – Away-From-Us
Both of Us – Felt the Pain
When-Your-Family – Moved-Away

Standing-There-Silent – The-Day-You-Left
Waving as You – Drove-Away
Watching – Holding-My-Breath

Life is so Funny and so Sad
Both of Us – Fell in Love-Again
Marrying the One – We-Loved
Only-Later to Fall – Out of Love

(Chorus)
Time Was Our Sadness
We Lived Our Lives
Remembering Each Other
Now Time Has Shined On Us
Letting Us Find Each Other
Midway Through Our Lives

Just-Like-That – It-Had to Be-Fate
We-Knew the Other-Instantly
We-Smiled – We-Hugged – We-Kissed
We-Wiped-Our – Tears-Away

In-Union – We-Said to The-Other
I-Love-You – Life's too Short
Let's-Live the Rest of Our-Lives
Together – In-Love as One
Yes-Was the Answer – As-We-Walked-Away-Free

(Chorus)
Time Was Our Sadness
We Lived Our Lives
Remembering Each Other
Now Time Has Shined On Us
Letting Us Find Each Other
Midway Through Our Lives

43

65. Stay

Leaving – Another – Lover
Can't-Help-It – It's-Not-Me
It's-All of Them
They-Never – Give-Me-That
Great-Big-L – Inside-My-Heart

It-Makes-Me-Sad and Lonely
Staying and Settling
Instead of Finding – True-Love
I-Know – If-I – Stay too Long
With-My – Non-True-Love
I'll-Never be Able to Find
The-One – That-Makes-My – Soul-Sing

(Chorus)
Why Won't You Stay
I Love You So Much
I'll Do Anything
If You Just Stay With Me
Is What I Hear – Every Time I Leave
To Find True Love

Am-I a Fool – In-Believing
I-Have the Ability – To-Find-True-Love
After-I – Failed so Many-Times
At-Falling in Love – Is-It-Out-There – If-It-Is
I'll-Find-It – I-Feel-This – In-My-Heart

It-Makes-Me-Sad to Stay and Settle
Instead of Finding – True-Love
I-Know – If-I – Stay too Long
With-My – Non-True-Love
I'll-Never be Able to Find
The-One – That-Makes-My – Soul-Sing

(Chorus)
Why Won't You Stay
I Love You So Much
I'll Do Anything
If You Just Stay With Me
Is What I Hear – Every Time I Leave
To Find True Love
44

Stay (What's The Point)

Baby – What's-Going-On
It's-Over – What a Blow to My-Heart
Yesterday was Great
Now-Today – You-Don't-Love-Me

What – Can – I – Say – But
Goodbye and Love-Sucks

(Chorus)
I Like To Ask Her To Stay
'Cause I Love Her
I Like To Ask Her To Stay
'Cause She Is Fine And Sexy
I Like To Ask Her To Stay
But What's The Point
As I Watch Her Ass – Walk Out My Door

It's-Raining – Inside-My-Heart
Storm-Clouds – Came-Rolling-In
When-She-Told-Me – I-Don't-Love-You
Now-I – Have to Sleep – Alone-Tonight

What – Can – I – Say – But
Love-Sucks – As it Attacks – My-Heart

(Chorus)
I Like To Ask Her To Stay
'Cause I Love Her
I Like To Ask Her To Stay
'Cause She Is Fine And Sexy
I Like To Ask Her To Stay
But What's The Point
As I Watch Her Ass – Walk Out My Door

Fare-Well-Love – You-Were-Nice
Really-Great for My-Heart and Body
What – Can – I – Say – But
Goodbye and Love-Sucks
What – Can – I – Say – But
Love-Sucks – As it Attacks – My-Heart

(Repeat Chorus)
45

66. High With Me

Baby-I'm High – Baby-I'm so High on Life
Let's-Go-Baby – Let's-Have a Great-Time
Life is Happening – I-Want to Feel-It
Sun or Rain – Snow or Rainbows
They-All-Feel so Good to Me

Sadly so Sadly – Your-Answer is No
Once-Again – You're-Down on Life
Baby-I-Wish – I-Could-Make-You – Smile
Baby-I-Wish – I-Could-Make-You – Love-Life

(Chorus)
Baby – I'm So Very High
Baby – You're So Very Low
I Love You Lots – But I Need A Lover
That Wants To Be High With Me
High With Me – While-Talking
High With Me – While-Laughing
High With Me While
Making-Love – Inside Or Outside

Baby-I'm High – Baby-I'm so High on Life
Let's-Go-Baby – Let's-Have a Great-Time
Life is Happening – I-Want to Feel-It
Sun or Rain – Snow or Rainbows
They-All-Feel so Good to Me

Sadly so Sadly – Your-Answer is No
Once-Again – You're-Down on Life
Baby-I-Wish – I-Could-Make-You – Smile
Baby-I-Wish – I-Could-Make-You – Love-Life

(Chorus)
Baby – I'm So Very High
Baby – You're So Very Low
I Love You Lots – But I Need A Lover
That Wants To Be High With Me
High With Me – While-Talking
High With Me – While-Laughing
High With Me While
Making-Love – Inside Or Outside

67. (I'm Busted) For I've Fallen In Love With You

We-Went-Out a Few-Times
Had-Some-Fun in Bed
It-Became-Apparent
It's-All-We-Had
It-Became-Apparent
That-We-Were-Sparkless

We-Said-Goodbye – Let's-Stay-Friends
We-Went-On – With-Our-Lives
Forgetting-About the-Other
Trying to Find – Some-Love for Our-Hearts

(Chorus)
We Promised That We'd
Take It One Day At A Time
But Now I'm Busted
For I've Fallen In Love With You
We Promised That We'd
Take It One Day At A Time
But Now I'm Busted
For I've Fallen In Love With You

Time-Slipped-By – As it Always-Does
Then-One-Day – There-You-Were
Walking-Up to Me – Looking-All-Pretty
By-The-End of The-Night
We-Were-In – Each-Other's-Arms
Kissing-Like – We-Needed a Release

Six-Months-Later – I-Was in Love
Six-Months-Later – I-Lied
Six-Months-Later – I'm-Busted

(Chorus)
We Promised That We'd
Take It One Day At A Time
But Now I'm Busted
For I've Fallen In Love With You
We Promised That We'd
Take It One Day At A Time
But Now I'm Busted
For I've Fallen In Love With You

47

68. Sweet Sweet Love

I-Tell-You-Folks
I-Was-Down and Out
Ready to Give it All-Up
Until-This – One-Night
When-I-Saw-This – Wonderful-Sight

This – Beautiful – Lady
Looking-Back at Me
It's-Been so Long
Too-Long – Not-To Feel
Squeeze and Hold – Someone-New

(Chorus)
'Cuz She's My – Sweet Sweet Love
You Know I Love My – Sweet Sweet Love
And I Always Will Love – My Sweet Sweet Love
'Cuz She's My – Sweet Sweet Love
You Know I Love My – Sweet Sweet Love
And I Always Will Love – My Sweet Sweet Love

I-Tell-You-Folks – I-Had-No-Idea
This-Hot and Beautiful-Lady
Was as Down and Out as I-Was
I-Gave-Her – What-She-Needed
While-She – Gave-Me-Mine

I-Made-Her – Smile and Flush
She-Made-Me – Shiver and Shake
We had Such a Great-Time
We-Fell in Love – For the Need
Of-Not-Being-Alone

(Chorus)
'Cuz She's My – Sweet Sweet Love
You Know I Love My – Sweet Sweet Love
And I Always Will Love – My Sweet Sweet Love
'Cuz She's My – Sweet Sweet Love
You Know I Love My – Sweet Sweet Love
And I Always Will Love – My Sweet Sweet Love

Sweet Love (That Sticks Around)

I-Tell-You-Folks
My-Sweet-Sweet-Love
Was so Fine – Then-She-Split
Left-Me for a Guy – That-Doesn't – Turn-Her-On
Go-Figure – Oh-Well – Did-I-Mention
She-Has a Sweet-Friend
That-Likes to Lick – My-Neck – Yeah-Right

(Pre-Chorus)
First Time Was Sweet-Sweet
Second-Time Is Sweet
Only Because I've Soured A Little-Bit
But That Don't Matter At All – Because

(Chorus)
She's My Sweet Love / That Turns Me On
She's My Sweet Love / That Likes To Be Turned On
She's My Sweet Love / That Sticks Around
She's My Sweet Love / And She Loves Me

I-Tell-You-Folks – I-Had-No-Idea
This-Hot and Beautiful-Friend
Was so Hot and Ready For-Love
I-Came a Calling to Her
For a Why-Not-Once
She-Showed-Me – That-Only-Sweet
Can be Very-Very – Sexy-Satisfying

(Pre-Chorus)
First Time Was Sweet-Sweet
Second-Time Is Sweet
Only Because I've Soured A Little Bit
But That Don't Matter At All – Because

(Chorus)
She's My Sweet Love / That Turns Me On
She's My Sweet Love / That Likes To Be Turned On
She's My Sweet Love / That Sticks Around
She's My Sweet Love / And She Loves Me

69. Pillow Talk

Love is Great
Everyone-That – Doesn't-Have-It
Is-Always – Searching for It
Making – Themselves – Miserable
That-They-Can't-Find
What so Many-Have

This-Thought – Can-Drive-You-Crazy
If-You-Let it Bring-You-Down
So-I-Say – Forget-About-Love
Have-Some – Sex-Instead
Least-You'll be Doing-Something
Even if You've-Had a Better-Time

(Chorus)
Sweet Thing That Was Just Pillow Talk
I Did Love You For A Moment
But After Deep Thought
I Liked What I Got
But I Have To Keep Our Thing
Strictly Pillow Talk
Hope You Understand – My Sweet Thing

I'm a Lady's-Man
Have it inside-Me to Make-Them-Purr
I'm-Such a Generous-Lover
Which-Makes-My – Sweet-Things
Very-Sad and Very-Mad
When-I-Walk – Out the Door

I-Can't-Help-Myself
This-Is-Who-I-Am
Best of All – I-Get to Do-This – To the Ladies
That—Can-Treat – All-Men – Like-Toys
Really-Blows – Their-Minds
When-They-Find-Out
That-I'm – Just-Like-Them

(Repeat Chorus)

Pillow Talk (I'm A Pillow Talker)

Ring-Ring – Hello
Well-Hello-Baby
How's-Your-Sweet-Body-Doing
What's-That – Sexy-Baby
Wow – You're-Hot – For a Date-Tonight

I-Don't-Know-Baby – I'm-Kinda-Busy
Tell-You-What – Sexy-Baby
Let-Me-Finish-Here
Then-I'll-Come-Over and Spend the Night

(Chorus)
Pillow Talk
The Ladies Love My Pillow Talk
I Pillow Talk Them – While They Loving Listen
Praying That I'll Pillow Talk Them
All Loving Night Long
Pillow Talk – I'm A Pillow Talker
That Never Hushes – Until I Pop

Ring-Ring – Hello
Well-Hello-Again-Baby
Is-Your-Sweet-Body-Still-Hot
What's-That – Sexy-Baby
Wow – You're-Hot – For-Another-Date

I-Can't-Baby – I'm-Busy
Tell-You-What – Sexy-Baby
I-Have to Finish-Here – Tonight
But at The-End of Tomorrow-Night
I'm – All – Yours

(Chorus)
Pillow Talk
The Ladies Love My Pillow Talk
I Pillow Talk Them – While They Loving Listen
Praying That I'll Pillow Talk Them
All Loving Night Long
Pillow Talk – I'm A Pillow Talker
That Never Hushes – Until I Pop

70. Summer Time And Love

Walking-Slowly in a Field
Of-Tall – Soft-Grass
I-Love the Summer-Time
Let it Stay – Summer-Forever

I'm in Love – She's so Hot-Love
She-Makes-Me-Feel so Welcome
Like-Coming-Home
Making-Love – Under the Stars
Raiding the Refrigerator
Falling-Asleep – Wrapped in Each-Other's-Arms
Summer-Time is Such a Blessing

(Chorus)
Summer Time And Love
What A Great Mixture
I'm Gonna Gobble Up
As Much Of It As I Can
Before Summer Time
Turns Into The Loneliness Of Winter

The-Starting of Coldness
Makes-You-Shiver
As-I-Put on My-Shoes
You-Want to Hibernate
Without-Me – Without-My-Love

Baby the Heat of My-Heart
Will-Make the Winter-Bearable
Let-Me-Stay – Loving-You – In the Cold
I'll-Bring – My-Summer to You
Keeping-You-Warm and Toasty
As-We-Watch the Snow-Fall

(Chorus)
Summer Time And Love
What A Great Mixture
I'm Gonna Gobble Up
As Much Of It As I Can
Before Summer Time
Turns Into The Loneliness Of Winter

52

Summer Time And Love (What A Great Mixture)

Walking-Slowly in a Field
Of-Tall – Soft-Grass
I-Love the Summer-Time
Let it Stay – Summer-Forever

I-Show-Up to You
With – Grass – Stained – Feet
Your-Smile – Makes-Me-Smile
Your – Love – High
Is-Shining so Very-Bright

(Chorus)
Summer Time And Love
What A Great Mixture
Summer Time And Love
Making Love In The Tall Grass
Summer Time And Love
I Never Want To Think Of Winter Again
Summer Time And Love
Only Comes Once A Year

Summer-Time-Lover
I-Had a Great-Time
Summer-Time-Lover
Let's-Follow the Sunshine
Summer-Time-Lover
Let's-Make-Love – Someplace-Else

I-Understand – Still it Makes-Me – Blue
How-About-This – Summer-Time-Lover
Next-Year – Same-Place – Same-Season

(Chorus)
Summer Time And Love
What A Great Mixture
Summer Time And Love
Making Love In The Tall Grass
Summer Time And Love
I Never Want To Think Of Winter Again
Summer Time And Love
Only Comes Once A Year

71. Happy Birthday Baby (Written 01-04-2014)
(For my Wife Christina – as a Surprise Birthday Present)

Today is Your-Day
So-Let's-Celebrate
Happy – Birthday – Baby
I-Hope-You – Have a Great-Day

If-You-Feel – Like-Being-Lazy
I'll-Lie-Down – With-You
If-You-Feel-Like – Hitting the Town
I'll-Be-Right-There – With-You
Loving-You – Because-You're-You

(Chorus)
Happy Birthday Baby
I Love You So much
The Only Aging I Can Tell
Is What's Inside My Heart
For You – My Loving Wife
So Happy Birthday Baby

You-Look so Beautiful-Today
I-Can't-Keep – My-Eyes-Off-You
Happy-Birthday-Baby
Wow is All – I-Can-Say
Pretty-Lady – I'm a Lucky-Man

Did-I-Tell-You – I-Love-You
Don't-Matter – One-Bit-Baby
Because – I'm-Going to Be
Whispering – I-Love-You
In-Your-Ears – All-Night-Long
As-I-Make – Sweet-Love to You

(Chorus)
Happy Birthday Baby
I Love You So much
The Only Aging I Can Tell
Is What's Inside My Heart
For You – My Loving Wife
So Happy Birthday Baby

I Only Dream Of You (868) (To Christina My Beautiful Wife)
(Written On Her Birthday January 06, 2016 – Finished 4:14 AM)

Hey-Baby – Hey-Darling
Hey-My-One and Only
I-Love-You – May-I-Have a Kiss
From-Your-Soft and Tender-Lips

Thanks-Baby – Thanks-Darling
Big-Heart-Stopper – Can-I-Have – Another
I-Love-You – I-Want-You
Can-I-Have – More-Than a Kiss
To-Help-Me – Sleep in Bliss

(Chorus)
I Only Dream Of You
Just You Baby – Just You Darling
I Only Dream Of You
Just You Baby – Just You Darling
I Only Dream Of You
Just You Baby – Just You Darling

Baby – Darling – When-I-Go to Sleep
I-Only-Dream of You – Because
You-Are-My-Dream – Come-True

Baby – Darling – When-I-Go to Sleep
I-Only-Dream of You – Because
I-Love-You – With-All-My-Heart

Baby – Darling – When-I-Go to Sleep
I-Only-Dream of You – Because
I-Do-Not-Want-Anybody-Else
Just-You-Baby – Just-You-Darling

(Chorus)
I Only Dream Of You
Just You Baby – Just You Darling
I Only Dream Of You
Just You Baby – Just You Darling
I Only Dream Of You
Just You Baby – Just You Darling

Happy Birthday Christina – I-Love-You (Times A Million And One)

72. She Let Me Pick Her

I – Was – Lonely
With-Plenty of Lovers
That's-All – They-Ever-Were
I-Enjoyed-Myself
Being-Lovers – Making-Love

But-In the Back of My-Mind
I-Knew – That-Wasn't-Enough
So-I-Had-My-Fun
While-Keeping – My-Eyes
Wide-Open – Looking for Love

(Chorus)
She Let Me Pick Her
I've Been So Lucky
She Said Yes To Me
She Let Me Pick Her
So We Could Make Together
A Great Life Forever

Told-Some-Lovers – I-Loved-Them
During-Hot – Burning-Passion
But-My-Heart – Told-Me
When-We-Were-Finished
That it Wasn't-True

I-Changed – My-Way of Thinking
I'm-Looking – For a Beautiful-Soul
That's-Inside a Beautiful-Woman
It-Took-Some-Time to Finally-Find
The-Special-Woman – Of-My-Dreams
The-Only-One – That-I-Could-Ever
Give-My-Heart-To

(Chorus)
She Let Me Pick Her
I've Been So Lucky
She Said Yes To Me
She Let Me Pick Her
So We Could Make Together
A Great Life Forever

73. Smile If You Love Me

I Like the Way – You-Make-Me-Feel
You-Got-Me – Thinking-About-You
All the Time – I'm-Lost
I'm-Under – Your-Control
And-You – Don't-Even-Know-It

That's-What – I-Love-About-You
All the Power – You-Have
All the Things – You-Could – Make-Me-Do
But-You're so Sweet and Loving
Making-Me – Want-You-Forever

(Chorus)
Passion Is Rising
Our Love Is Soaring High
All You Have To Do Is
Smile If You Love Me
And I'd Marry You – Right Now

You-Smile – Then-You-Pause
My-Love for You
Came to You – Really-Fast
Sent-You – Into-Over-Thinking
Not-Knowing – What to Do

I-Calm-You – With a Kiss
You-Look – Into-My-Eyes
Then-You – Smile at Me
Saying-Yes – I-Love-You
I'll-Be-Yours – Forever

(Chorus)
Passion Is Rising
Our Love Is Soaring High
All You Have To Do Is
Smile If You Love Me
And I'd Marry You – Right Now

(Brand new song that I wrote for this Book. I took away the line Smile if you Love me from another song and came up with these lyrics.)

57

74. Makes Me Smile

I-Feel so Down
Life is Kicking-Me – Around
I'm-All – Into-My-Sadness
When-You-Walk – Up to Me
With a Smile – On-Your-Face

You-Give-Me a Hug and a Kiss
Making-Me – Feel-Better
Letting the Fact – You-Love-Me
Clear-Out – My-Sadness
Making a Smile – Appear on My-Face
Making-Me – Want to Say

(Chorus)
Hello Darling – I Love You – I Need You
Thank You For Being – My One And Only
The One That Always – Makes Me Smile
Hello Darling – I Love You – I Need You
Thank You For Being – My One And Only
The One That Always – Makes Me Smile

You're so Up and Go
Won't-Let-Me-Stay
All-Bottled-Up-Inside
You-Know – What-I-Need
And-I-Let-You – Show-Me

Passion in Your-Eyes
Love in Your-Voice
As-You-Hug and Kiss-Me-Longer
Bringing-Me-Around – Even-More
Making-Me – Want to Say

(Chorus)
Hello Darling – I Love You – I Need You
Thank You For Being – My One And Only
The One That Always – Makes Me Smile
Hello Darling – I Love You – I Need You
Thank You For Being – My One And Only
The One That Always – Makes Me Smile

58

75. It's Time For Love

Turn-Your-Frown – Upside-Down
You-Sad-Sack of Non-Caring
As-You-Sit-There – All-Alone
Waiting for Something to Happen

Believe-Me – When-I-Say
There's-Somebody – Out-There
Waiting-For-You to Find-Them
So-Get-Up and Fire-Up – Your-Love

(Chorus)
It's Time For Love
Wishing You Weren't Alone
Does No Good At All
You Have To Want To Say
No More Of This
And Go Find Somebody To Love
Because My Friend
It's Time For Love

I-Come-Back to You
To-See if You – Found-Love
All-I-See is Your
Same – Stubborn – Frown

It's-Still-Hanging-Around
Keeping-You – All-Alone
Preventing-Love – From-Finding-You
So-I-Snap – My-Fingers
And-Say to You – Once-Again

(Chorus)
It's Time For Love
Wishing You Weren't Alone
Does No Good At All
You Have To Want To Say
No More Of This
And Go Find Somebody To Love
Because My Friend
It's Time For Love

76. Let's Be Friends (That Sleep Together)

My-Friend-Calls-Me
Another-Lover – Has-Left-Her
She's-Crying the I'm-All-Alone
Come-Over and Talk to Me
Because – I-Need-You

I-Have to Be – Her-Rock
That-She-Can – Lean-On
Agreeing to Let – My-Shirt-Get-Wet
From-All-The-Tears – She'll-Be-Crying

(Chorus)
Let's Be Friends That Sleep Together
I'm Still Alone
Now You Are Again
So Dry Your Eyes
I Have A Great Idea
Let's Be Friends That Sleep Together

My-Pretty-Friend – I've-Known for Years
Looks at Me so Surprised – I'm-Standing
Above-Her – With-My-Hand-Out
She-Closes – Her-Mouth and Smiles
Then-She-Gives-Me – Her-Hand

We-Look – Each-Other in the Eyes
Saying-Yes – To a Night-Together
Both of Us-Shaking – Wanting to Say-No
But-Our-Loneliness – Is so Heavy
We-Bit-Our-Tongues and Let-Ourselves-Go

(Chorus)
Let's Be Friends That Sleep Together
I'm Still Alone
Now You Are Again
So Dry Your Eyes
I Have A Great Idea
Let's Be Friends That Sleep Together

The-Silence – That-Came-After
Was-Not – That-Heavy – After-All
As-We-Put – Our-Clothes-Back-On
Staring-Silently – Then-Laughing
As-We-Talked at the Same-Time
Both of Saying the Same-Thing

(Chorus)
Let's Be Friends That Sleep Together
I'm Still Alone
Now You Are Again
So Dry Your Eyes
I Have A Great Idea
Let's Be Friends That Sleep Together

We are Happy and Doing-Great
Finding a Release – That-We – Both-Needed
We are Not in Love and Not-Trying to Be
Both of Us-Know – That-Love-Sucks
And-What-We-Have - is - Something-Very-Special

Being-Friends – That-Sleep-Together
Is-Wild and Very-Different
Especially – When-Our – Sleeping-Friend
Has a Date – With-Another
That the Other – Doesn't-Want – Them to Have
Getting-Embarrassed – When-Reminded
This-Thing – We-Have is Not-Love
It's – Just – Sex

(Chorus)
Let's Be Friends That Sleep Together
I'm Still Alone
Now You Are Again
So Dry Your Eyes
I Have A Great Idea
Let's Be Friends That Sleep Together

77. Forget About Our Love

After a Few-Years of Being
The-Friends – That-Sleep-Together
We're-Calling-It-Quits
We're – Still – Friends
No-More-Touching – Just-Talking
When-We-Get-Together

Sometimes a Brush – Against-Flesh
Lights a Spark – That-Burns-Quickly
We-Back-Up and Smile
Looking at The-Other
Neither of Us-Daring
To-Say – What's-On – Our-Minds

(Chorus)
You Can Have Him – I'll Take Her
Both Of Us Needs This
So Both Of Us Can Go On
Trying To Forget About Our Love
That We Shared Together

We're-Double-Dating
She-Likes-Him – I-Hate-Him
I-Like-Her – She-Hates-Her
Don't-Know – What's-Her-Problem
My-Date is Really-Hot
Hers-However is a Real-Dud

I-Feel-Sorry for My-Friend
Wearing-Her – Sexy-Green-Dress
With-No-One to Appreciate – The-Extra-Time
She-Took to Make-Herself
Look so Amazing – Tonight

(Chorus)
You Can Have Him – I'll Take Her
Both Of Us Needs This
So Both Of Us Can Go On
Trying To Forget About Our Love
That We Shared Together

I-Don't-Like – What's-Going-On
My-Friend – Needs-Her-Friend
I'm-Going to Change-Things – Back
To the Way – We-Use to Be
The-Way – We-Were-Meant to Be

No-Longer – Friends that Sleep-Together
No – From-Now-On and Forever
We'll be Known as
The-Lovers – That-Love the Other

I-Break – My-Silence
Telling-My-Friend and Lover
To-Come-Over and Sit on My-Lap
She-Closes-Her-Mouth and Smiles
She-Sits on My-Lap and Gives-Me
My – I-Still-Love-You – Kiss

(Chorus)
You Can Have Him – I'll Take Her
Both Of Us Needs This
So Both Of Us Can Go On
Trying To Forget About Our Love
That We Shared Together

Years-Later – We-Both-Still-Laugh – On the Night
We-Found-Out – That-We-Were Being – Such-Fools
Realizing-With-That – Special-Kiss
We-Were-Made to Be-Together

Walking-Out – Holding-Hands
After-We-Told – Our-Dates so Long
Not-Caring – How-We-Seemed to Them
Only-Thing – That-Mattered to Us
Was-Making – Our-Temperatures-Rise

(Chorus)
You Can Have Him – I'll Take Her
Both Of Us Needs This
So Both Of Us Can Go On
Trying To Forget About Our Love
That We Shared Together

78. Turn Me On Baby

Life is Turning-Me – Off
Everywhere is Lost
Everybody is So-Down
From the Heavy of The-World
There-Seems to Be – No-More-Fun

I-Got-You – You-Got-Me
We-Fell in Love so Fast
The-World-Stopped-Turning
While-We-Were – Making-Love
When-We-Slowed-Down – We-Were-Older
The-World had Changed
And-We-Didn't – Even-Notice

(Chorus)
Turn Me On Baby / I Need Some Comfort
The Feel Of Your Passion / And All Of Your Love
Turn Me On Baby / I Need Some Comfort
The Feel Of Your Passion / And All Of Your Love

Day by Day – Our-Big-Time-Love
Keeps-Us – Safe and Sound
As the World – Turns so Cold
We-Still-Feel – Beauty In Her
Letting-Us-Know – That-There's
Still-Hope – Within-Us-All

We-Can't – Change the World
We-Are-Only – Two-People in Love
We-Will-Stay-This-Way
As-Long as We – Don't-Let
The-World – Change-Our-Love

(Chorus)
Turn Me On Baby / I Need Some Comfort
The Feel Of Your Passion / And All Of Your Love
Turn Me On Baby / I Need Some Comfort
The Feel Of Your Passion / And All Of Your Love

Let Me (Turn You On)

What's-Up – Check-Out – What-Always-Works
I-Think – I-Know –One of Your-Friends
She's the Hot-One
Almost as Hot as You
You-Like-That – Darling

Well-Darling – Let-Me
Turn – You – On
Then-You-Can – Thank-Me
In the Morning-Light
By-Inviting-Me – Back-Over – Tomorrow-Night

(Chorus)
Oh-Baby – Oh-Darling
Let Me Turn You On
You'll Love It – I Promise
Oh-Baby – Oh-Darling
Let Me Turn You On
I'm Primed And Ready
For A Love Making Time

What's-Up – Check-Out – What-Always-Works
I-Think – I-Know –One of Your-Friends
She's the Hot-One
Almost as Hot as You
You-Like-That – Darling

Well-Darling – Let-Me
Turn – You – On
Then-You-Can – Thank-Me
In the Morning-Light
By-Inviting-Me – Back-Over – Tomorrow-Night

(Chorus)
Oh-Baby – Oh-Darling
Let Me Turn You On
You'll Love It – I Promise
Oh-Baby – Oh-Darling
Let Me Turn You On
I'm Primed And Ready
For A Love Making Time

79. She Still Has That Body

My-Adored-One
We've-Loved-Together so Great
All-These-Long-Years
I'm so Grateful for That
You-Loved-Me – When-I was Nice
You-Loved-Me – When-I was Not
Your-Love – Gives-Me-Strength
Now-I'm-Ready for Some-More

(Chorus)
She Still Has That Body – That Still Drives Me Crazy
Even After All These Years – I Know I Still Got It So Good
She Still Has That Body – That Still Drives Me Crazy
Even After All These Years – I Know I Still Got It So Good

Your-Smile – That-You-Give-Me
After-We-Make-Love
Drives-Me – Happy-Confident
That-You-Still – Want-Me
I-Love-When-You – Chew on My-Lips
When-I'm-Squeezing – Your-Hips
Loving-I-Can-Still – Turn-You-On
With-My-Sweet-Hot – Pillow-Talk

(Chorus)
She Still Has That Body – That Still Drives Me Crazy
Even After All These Years – I Know I Still Got It So Good
She Still Has That Body – That Still Drives Me Crazy
Even After All These Years – I Know I Still Got It So Good

Years – Take-Their-Toll – On-Lovers
By-Looking at Us
You'll – Never – Know
Because – We-Were so Strong
The-Hard – Went-Away-Eventually
As-The-Good – Stayed-Around
And-Through it All – We-Made-Love
While-Staying in Love

(Repeat Chorus)

66

Sexy Bodies (Look At That Sexy Body)

I'm-All-Man
I-Get-Loving-All the Time
But-I – Have to Stop and Say
Look-At-That – Sexy-Body
Wow – Do-I-Want-To
Lay-Down – With-That-Sexy-Body

Then-Again – Look at That
Even-Sexier-Body – Over-There
Tonight is Going to Be
A-Great-Night – My-Friend

(Chorus)
Forget-Love – Think-Sex
For Everywhere – My Friend
Are Sexy Bodies To Look At
Forget-Love – Think-Sex
For Everywhere – My Friend
Are Sexy Bodies / Waiting To Be Enjoyed
By-Me – And By You – Let's-Go-Get-'Em

I'm-All-Man
I-Get-Loving-All the Time
But-I – Have to Stop and Say
Look-At-That – Sexy-Body
Wow – Do-I-Want-To
Lay-Down – With-That-Sexy-Body

Then-Again – Look at That
Even-Sexier-Body – Over-There
Tonight is Going to Be
A-Great-Night – My-Friend

(Chorus)
Forget-Love – Think-Sex
For Everywhere – My Friend
Are Sexy Bodies To Look At
Forget-Love – Think-Sex
For Everywhere – My Friend
Are Sexy Bodies / Waiting To Be Enjoyed
By-Me – And By You – Let's-Go-Get-'Em

80. Lady From Space (Love Version)

I-Know-Her-Name
I-Can-Understand – Her-Speech
But-I-Can't – Understand-Why
For-What-I'm – Looking-At
Is a Lady-From-Space

She's-Dresses in Such a Pretty-Dress
Looking-Like – Such a Sweet and Nice
Space-Lady to Have a Talk-With
She is so Beautiful-Looking
With-Her – Purple and Pink – Space-Body

(Chorus)
She's Not From Around Here
She's A Lady From Space
Out For A Weekend – Love Exploring Space
She's Not Interested In Sex
She's Only Interested In Great Love
So I Said Yes And She Space Kissed Me

I-Invite this Space-Beauty
Inside – My – Home
She is Lonely – She is Sad
I-Make-Us – Some-Tea and Coffee
We-Drink as She – Tells-Me – Her-Story

This-Good-Looking and Loving
Space-Lady – Is-In-Need of Love
I-Take-A-Hold – Of-Two-Of-Her – Four-Hands
Pulling-Her in For a Great-Big-Hug
Then-Like a Earth-Friend – I-Earth-Kissed Her

(Chorus)
She's Not From Around Here
She's A Lady From Space
Out For A Weekend – Love Exploring Space
She's Not Interested In Sex
She's Only Interested In Great Love
So I Said Yes And She Space Kissed Me

Wow! – What a Night – I-Had-Last-Night
I'll-Never-Be the Same – Again
Earth-Women – Are so Very-Loving
But-Compared to My – Space-Lady
They-Are – Two-Arms – Too-Short

They-Don't-Have – That-Special-Voice
That-Drives-Me – Loving-Crazy
Making-Me-Feel and Act-Like – I'm the Greatest
Human-Man – That-Ever-Lived

(Chorus)
She's Not From Around Here
She's A Lady From Space
Out For A Weekend – Love Exploring Space
She's Not Interested In Sex
She's Only Interested In Great Love
So I Said Yes And She Space Kissed Me

My-Lady from Space is Named-Krie
Krie's – Planet is Called-Flith
Next-Month – Krie's-Coming-Back to Earth
Next-Month – I'm-Leaving-Earth

My-Lady from Space is Named-Krie
Best of All – Krie-Lied-About-Sex
Best of All – We're-Lovers
Best of All – We're-Still-Friends

My-Lady from Space is Named-Krie
Best of All – Krie is Rich
Best of All – Krie-Likes to Party
Best of All – Krie-Has a Lot of Friends
Best of All – I'll-Be the Only-Human on Flith
Best of All – Wait a Minute

(Chorus)
She's Not From Around Here
She's A Lady From Space
Out For A Weekend – Love Exploring Space
She's Not Interested In Sex
She's Only Interested In Great Love
So I Said Yes And She Space Kissed Me

Dear Love,
Thank you for Showing me
How to Love Someone again,
It has Been so Long for me.
I thought my Heart had Hardened,
But Thankfully I was Wrong.
I Love You – See You Soon.

Dear Love,
I hope you enjoy the Lunch I packed for you
It is Full of Things I know you Like.
I can't Wait for you to come Home
So I can Show you things I know you Love
And We can have a Great night.
Have a great day, I love you

Dear Love,
All I can Say to You
Is I've had Enough of Your Constant Flirting.
It might Seem Fun and Harmless to You
But it is Tearing At my Soul.
I can't help Feeling That You're Not Satisfied with me,
why else would you constantly do this every time we go out.
I've had enough, this needs to end, if you're not happy then
leave me.

Dear Love,
Even After all of these Years
Every time I look at Your Sweet Face
My Heart still Beats so Hard, Fast and True for You.
Tomorrow is just Another Day this is True
But with You in My Life it is another Day I'm Looking Forward to.
I Love You, I Need You, I can't wait to make love to you.

(Demos) (Pages 71-97)

(Book Three)

Little By Little (Duet)

Push Me Away

Ordinary

Love

A Beautiful Woman

The Lovers Of Forever

(Book Four)

She's Got To Be Mine

Love Baby Love

High With Me

Lady From Space
(8 Page Lyrical Story Version)

Little By Little (Duet) (Demo Version)

(Her)
We're so New-Together
I-Don't-Even-Know – Your-Favorite-Color
Our-Infatuations – Are-Blooming
It's-All-About – Looks-Right-Now
My-Wants – My-Needs – Are-Pulling-Me-Closer
Making-Me – Want to Lose-Control

(Chorus)
(Together) Little By Little
(Her) Let's Take Our Time
(Him) Little By Little
(Her) Let's See What Happens
(Him) Little By Little
(Her) Maybe We'll Fall In Love
(Him) Little By Little
(Together) Little By Little

(Him)
Taking-Our-Time is Kinda-Cool
But-Baby – My-Passion is Burning
I-Want-You so Bad – Pretty-Lady
Every-Time – I-See-You – You-Look
Even-Better – Than the Time-Before
Baby-If-You-Ask – My-Heart – Right-Now
It-Would – Tell-You this Baby
I-Will-Fall in Love – With-You-While
We're-Making-Love – For the Fist-Time

(Chorus)
(Together) Little By Little
(Her) Let's Take Our Time
(Him) Little By Little
(Her) Let's See What Happens
(Him) Little By Little
(Her) Maybe We'll Fall In Love
(Him) Little By Little
(Together) Little By Little

(Her)
You're-What – I-Want-In a Man
But-I-Have the Feeling – That-You'll-Take
Then-Leave – Making-Me-Hate-You so Much
That-I-Gave-You – What-You-Wanted
Instead of Making-You-Wait – 'Til-You-Loved-Me

(Him)
Baby-Love is a Chance
I-Want-It – I-Think – I-Need-It
But-I-Can't-Wait – Much-Longer
I-Can't-Give – My-Heart to You
Until-I – Have a Taste of Your-Flame
That-Way – You and I – Will-Know
If-We-Fit – Just-Right-Together

(Chorus)
(Together) Little By Little
(Her) Let's Take Our Time
(Him) Little By Little
(Her) Let's See What Happens
(Him) Little By Little
(Her) Maybe We'll Fall In Love
(Him) Little By Little
(Together) Little By Little

(Her) We're so New-Together
(Him) Taking-Our-Time is Kinda-Cool
(Her) Our-Infatuations – Are-Blooming
(Him) I-Want-You so Bad-Pretty-Lady
(Her) You're-What – I-Want-In a Man
(Him) Baby-Love is a Chance

(Chorus)
(Together) Little By Little
(Her) Let's Take Our Time
(Him) Little By Little
(Her) Let's See What Happens
(Him) Little By Little
(Her) Maybe We'll Fall In Love
(Him) Little By Little
(Together) Little By Little

Push Me Away (Demo Version)

Can't-Believe – It's-Been-This-Long
I-Miss-You so Much – I-Feel-It
Rolling-Over – You're-Not-There
Your-Scent is Almost-Gone
If-We – Let this Goes-On
It will Become a Memory

Do-You-Really – Want to Take the Chance
That-Our-Love – Will-Fade-Away
What a Shame All-I-Can-Say
I-Want to Hold – Squeeze and Love-You
If-You – Come-Back to Me
Oh-Baby – I'll-Never-Stop

Love-Is – What-I-Have
I-Will be Your-Everything
You-Can-Depend on Me
The Laughs – The-Tears
I-Will-Be-There for You

(Chorus)
If You Have To Push Me Away
To Have Your Space
To Feel Your Freedom
Push Me Away
'Cause Baby I'm Here To Stay
I'll Take It For Us – Push Me Away
If You Have To – Do It And Come Back

I-Will-Still-Love-You – When-You-Come-Back
You-Pushed – I-Stayed – Out of Sight
Waiting for Our-Love to Continue-On
Push-Me-Away – All-You-Want
I-Know-Deep-Down – That-You-Love-Me
And-You-Want to Come-Back to Me
Makes-Me-Forever – Love-You – Even-More

You-Re-Enter-My-Life – All-You-Have to Do
Is-Look at Me – Your-Eyes are So-Loving
You-Kiss-Me so Deep – You-Hug-Me so Tight
I'm-Here for You – Once-Again

74

Just-Lean-On – Down-Upon-Me
I'll-Keep-You-Safe and Warm
Knowing-Baby – I'm-Your-One
Seeing in Your-Eyes – That-You are Sorry

I-Know-Baby
You-Don't-Have to Say-It
Just-Being – Your-Man – Once-Again
Is-All-That-I-Need to Make-Me-Happy

(Chorus)
If You Have To Push Me Away
To Have Your Space
To Feel Your Freedom
Push Me Away
'Cause Baby I'm Here To Stay
I'll Take It For Us – Push Me Away
If You Have To – Do It And Come Back

Maybe-You-Think – That-You
Pushed-Me-Away – For-Too-Long
I'm – Still – Solid
Held-Together by Our-Love

Now's the Time – You-Feel
That-We-Should – Stay-Together
No-More – Pushing-Me-Away
You-Keep-Me – Very-Close
It's so Different for You
Now-That-You-Feel
You-Have-Something to Lose

I 'm-Now – Your-Somebody
That-You-Don't-Mind
Telling – Everybody – About
Through-Me and My-Love
You-Have-Found – Your-Love for Me
And it Will – Last-Forever
Just-Like – My-Love for You

(Repeat Chorus)

75

Ordinary (Demo Version)

She's a Waitress
At a Local-Bar
That-Brightens it Up
For-Everyone-There
Every-Man has Asked-Twice
To-Be the One to Be with Her

She's-Not-Interested
She's-Nice – About-It and Likes-It
But it's Always a Big-No
She's so Beautiful
She's the Kinda-Woman
That-Any-Man – Would-Want – For a Wife

(Chorus)
She Might Think She's Ordinary
Not Giving It Much Thought
Even Though Men Are Always Asking
She Just Smiles And Says No
She'd Rather Be By Herself
For Alone Is Comfortable
It's Her Ordinary

She-Dresses so Sexy
She-Has-To it's Part of The-Job
But that Doesn't – Bother-Her
She-Wears it With-Pride
She-Knows – She-Has a Great-Body
And-She-Likes to Have a Great-Time

Dancing-Herself to Your-Table
Bringing-You-Drinks – That-You
Can't-Even – Pay-Attention to
'Cause – She's so Fine
When-You – Look-Her in Her-Eyes
All-You-See - is - Yes-I-Know
How-Much – You-Want-Me
So-Give-Me a Big-Hard-Tip
As-My-Tail – Walks-Away – Telling-You-No

(Chorus)
She Might Think She's Ordinary
Not Giving It Much Thought
Even Though Men Are Always Asking
She Just Smiles And Says No
She'd Rather Be By Herself
For Alone Is Comfortable
It's Her Ordinary

Leaving – Drinking just Enough
Walking-Along – Feeling-Good
There-She is Standing-There
The-Lady of My-Dreams
Getting-Closer to Say-Hello
I-Notice – She is Crying – Trying to Hide-It

I-Ask-Her if I-Can – Help-Her-Out
Rose – Wipes-Her-Eyes
And-Says-No – I'm-Fine
I-Smile and say Goodnight
Walking-Away – Rose-Says to Me – Wait
Turning-Around – Hoping-Praying

The-Lady of My-Dreams
Walks-Up to Me and Gives-Me a Kiss
Rose-Stops – Looks-Me-Straight in My-Eyes
And-Says – With a Spark in Her-Eyes
He's-Not-Coming-Back
I'm-Tired of Waiting
Since-You've-Been so Nice to Me
And-I'm – In the Need of Some-Lovin'
If-You're-Gentle – You-Can-Have-Me

(Chorus)
She Might Think She's Ordinary
Not Giving It Much Thought
Even Though Men Are Always Asking
She Just Smiles And Says No
She'd Rather Be By Herself
For Alone Is Comfortable
It's Her Ordinary

Love (Demo Version)

I-Awake – With-You in My-Arms
Your-Softness – Feels so Good
We-Are so Close and In-Love
I-Grab-You and Pull-You-Closer
So-I-Can – Feel-You-Even-More

You-Stir in My-Arms
Scooting-Closer to Me
Moaning-How-Good – I-Feel to You
Smiling – Starting to Lightly-Wake
Then-Giving-Me – My-Morning-Kiss
Falling-Back to Sleep
As-Soon as You-Lay
Your-Head on My-Chest

(Chorus)
Love – Is What We Have
Love – Is Our Everything
Love – Keeps Us In Love
Love – Together Forever

We-Shower-Together – I-Can't-Keep
My-Hands-Off-You – You-Tell-Me to Stop
I-Laugh and Do-It – Some-More
You-Swat – My-Hands-Away
Telling-Me-Off – And
Kissing-Me – At the Same-Time

We-Have-Our – Morning-Together
Doing-Our-Things so We-Can-Leave
Having-Our – Separate-Days
Always – Calling – Midday
Just to Hear the Other's-Voice
We-Hang-Up – With an I-Love-You

(Chorus)
Love – Is What We Have
Love – Is Our Everything
Love – Keeps Us In Love
Love – Together Forever

Evenings – Go so Fast
Never-Enough – Time-Together
Always-Waiting – For the Time
When-We – Go to Bed – To-Make-Love

Trying to Take – Our-Time
Enjoying – What-We-Have
What-We've-Shared – For so Long
Happy – Together – Forever
Not-Wanting – Anyone-Else
But – Each – Other

(Chorus)
Love – Is What We Have
Love – Is Our Everything
Love – Keeps Us In Love
Love – Together Forever

Might-Be the Same – Everyday
We-Don't-Mind – We-Love-It
Together – We-Can – Handle-Anything
That-Comes-Our-Way – Due to Our-Love

Through the Years – Our-Love's – Been-Tested
Passing-Every-Time – With-Lovely-Colors
Even the Bad and the Mad – We-Give-Out
Goes-Away – It-Might-Leave-Scars
But-Our-Love is Strong
Helping to Heal – Our-Life's-Wounds

(Chorus)
Love – Is What We Have
Love – Is Our Everything
Love – Keeps Us In Love
Love – Together Forever

A Beautiful Woman (Demo Version)

Looks-Are so Important
It's-What – Turns-Us-On
That-Moment of Hot-Passion
That-Turns-Gray – Into-Blue

We-All-Want-Love
But it Comes-Around so Slow
Making-Us – Not-Pay-Attention
To the Chance – That-We-Just-Lost
While-Coasting-By – Without-Even-Noticing-It
And-I'm-Tired of Playing it Slow

(Chorus)
A Beautiful Woman
Is a Beautiful Woman
If You're Lucky Enough
To Have One Enter Your Life
You Have To Give Her – A Honest Love
Not A Love – That Will Smother Her

You're so Lonely – Without-Love
She's-Looking at You – With-That-Smile
You've-Seen so Many-Times
But-This-Time – It-Seems-Different
The-Girl – Next-Door to You
Who's-Always-Only – Been-Your-Friend

She's-Not a Model – She's a Beautiful-Woman
That-You – Get-Along-With
She's-Seen-You-Sick – She's-Seen-You-Ugly
She-Smells so Nice – She-Looks so Pretty
With a Figure – You-Notice
That-Looks – Twice as Nice
Makes-You-Want to Be – More-Than-Friends

(Chorus)
A Beautiful Woman
Is a Beautiful Woman
If You're Lucky Enough
To Have One Enter Your Life
You Have To Give Her – A Honest Love
Not A Love – That Will Smother Her

(Chorus)
A Beautiful Woman
Is a Beautiful Woman
If You're Lucky Enough
To Have One Enter Your Life
You Have To Give Her – A Honest Love
Not A Love – That Will Smother Her

Your-Long-Time-Friend
Is-Looking at You
With-Surprised – Brown-Eyes
Of-What-Are-You-Doing
She's-Not – Interested in You
She-Loves-You – As a Friend
You-Feel – Like-Such a Fool

Embarrassingly – You-Walk-Away
Turning too Quickly
Bumping-Into the Most
Beautiful-Woman – You've-Ever-Seen
You-Stand-There – With-Your-Heart
Hanging-Out to Her

She-Smiles and Says-Hello
Thank-You – For-Bumping-Into-Me
I'm-All-Alone and I'm-Looking
For-Someone to Talk to
Is-This-You – Mister-Just
Standing-There and Staring at Me

(Chorus)
A Beautiful Woman
Is a Beautiful Woman
If You're Lucky Enough
To Have One Enter Your Life
You Have To Give Her – A Honest Love
Not A Love – That Will Smother Her

The Lovers Of Forever (Demo Version)

I'm in Love – She's in Love with Me
We're-Doing-Great
Can't-Believe – It's so Simple
Seems-Everybody's – Having-Trouble
But-Not-Us - We're-Doing-Fine

Everything is Falling into Place
Both of Us – Are-Ready
To-Take that Next-Step
So-I-Ask-My-Love to Marry-Me
She-Cries and Says-Yes
To-Being-Mine – Forever

(Chorus)
I Love Her
I Know I Shouldn't
Because I Belong To Another
But I Can't Help Myself
For We Are The Lovers Of Forever
And We Just Found Each Other Again

I-Call-My-Love to Tell-Her – I-Love-Her
Hang-Up – I'm-Going to Marry-Her
This-Thought – Makes-Me – Feel so Good
For-I-Have – No-Reason to Doubt – Anything
We're-Going to Make-It – That is All

I-Get a Little-Thirsty from Thinking
I-Enter this Crowded-Bar
Order a Bourbon and Cola
Drinking-Half of it Down – I-Turn-Around
Seeing the Love of My-Lives
Staring-Back at Me so Lovingly

We-Don't – Know-Each-Other-Yet
All it Takes is One-Look
We-Found-Out – Instantly
We've-Been in Love-Before

(Chorus)
I Love Her
I Know I Shouldn't
Because I Belong To Another
But I Can't Help Myself
For We Are The Lovers Of Forever
And We Just Found Each Other Again

She-Has – Such-Bright-Eyes
I-Lose-Myself in Them
I-Cannot – Help-It
They're so Heavenly
I-Just-Stand-There
Looking-Deep into Them
Wishing to Myself – I-Was
Marrying-Her – Instead of My-Love

My-Heart – My-Soul – Tells-Me
This-Special-Lady – I'm-Holding
Is-My – Forever-Love
Thoughts of My-Betrayal
Hurts-Me – Very-Deep
What-Can-I-Do
I-Still-Love – My-Love
But-I-Just-Found – My-Forever-Love

With-Happiness in My-Mind
With-Sadness in My-Voice
I-Take a Walk to Call-Back – My-Love
To-End – Our-Future-Together
Walking-Back – Taking a Deep-Breath
Readying-Myself – For the Rekindling
Of-Love – Space and Time
As the Lovers of Forever
Meet-Again – For the First-Time

(Chorus)
I Love Her
I Know I Shouldn't
Because I Belong To Another
But I Can't Help Myself
For We Are The Lovers Of Forever
And We Just Found Each Other Again

83

She's Got To Be Mine (Demo Version)

Standing-Apart – In a Crowd
We've-Been-Feeling – Each-Other
A-Connection – Was-Felt
When-Our – Eyes-Met
Familiarity-Sinking-In
As-You-Kept-On – Walking-By
When-You – First-Entered the Party

We are Staring – Neither of Us
Wanting to Be the First-One
To-Make-First-Contact
Fear – Overwhelment
Keeps-Us – Safely-Apart

(Chorus)
She's Got To Be Mine
Just Look At Her
She's So Sweet And Hot
I Want To Love Her
For A Very Long Time

Both of Us are Getting-Spent
So-Very-Taxing – Holding-Back the Urge
To-Walk-Up and Say-Hello to Our-Destiny
Feeling the Ice – Start to Melt in My-Body
Smiling – I-Know-Already
That-Our-Time – Will-Be-Coming-Soon

I-Can-Tell – That-You're-Not
Into the Guy – You're-With
Seeing in Me – That-I-Want-You
Instead – Of the Two-Ladies
That are Talking to Me

(Chorus)
She's Got To Be Mine
Just Look At Her
She's So Sweet And Hot
I Want To Love Her
For A Very Long Time

We've-Had-Enough
Turning to Face – Each-Other
Leaving-Our-Group – Behind
We-Walk in Union – To the Center of The-Room
Stopping a Whisper's-Breath – From the Other
To-Stare – Into-Each-Other's-Souls

Grabbing – One – Another
Feeling-What – We-Already-Know
We-Go-In for That – Releasing-First-Kiss
Passion-Unfolds – As-We-Connect

(Chorus)
She's Got To Be Mine
Just Look At Her
She's So Sweet And Hot
I Want To Love Her
For A Very Long Time

Standing-Apart – In a Crowd
We've-Been-Feeling – Each-Other
A-Connection – Was-Felt
When-Our – Eyes-Met
Familiarity-Sinking-In
As-You-Kept-On – Walking-By
When-You – First-Entered the Party

Stopping-Kissing – We-Just-Smile
As-Everybody is Watching
Us-Hold-Hands – Walking-Out-Together
To-Start – Our-First-Day
That-Will-Lead – All the Way
To the End of Our-Lives

(Chorus)
She's Got To Be Mine
Just Look At Her
She's So Sweet And Hot
I Want To Love Her
For A Very Long Time

Love Baby Love (Demo Version)

Hello-Baby – It's-Me
I-Thought-I'd-Try
One-More-Time
To-Let-You-Know
That-I'm the Real-Thing

This-Time it's Love
Comin' for You
Not a One-Time – Or
'Til-I'm-Bored
I-Look at You
I-Feel – Weak-All-Over

I'll-Be-Amazed – Every-Day
You – Are – Mine
So-Happy-I'll-Be – That-My-Love
Will-Shine-Down on You
Then-You – Will-Understand
I'm the One – For-You

(Pre-Chorus)
Please Just Notice Me
Give Me Just One Chance
I Will Be So Good For You
You'll Never Have To Look For Love Again

(Chorus)
Love Baby Love
That's What I Have For You
Love Baby Love
You Need It I Can Tell
Love Baby Love
Give Into It – It Will Never Stop
Love Baby Love
You Can Look Everywhere
And Never Find One So True
Love Baby Love
That's What I Have For You

Years – Yes-Years – Have-Passed-By
You-Still – Shine so Bright
I'm so Glad – That-You – Took-My-Love
And-Gave-It to Yourself

It-Helped-You-Along
So-You – Could-Give-Me
Your-Sweet-Love
You-Had – Deep-Inside-You
It-Might – Have-Been-Misplaced
Thankfully – It-Was-Not-Lost

I-Still-Kneel – To-Our – Altar of Love
I-Would've-Sacrificed – Anything for You
I-Know-You-Know – This as Truth
We-Have the True-One-Love
Everybody-Else – Will-Never-Have
'Cause-Heaven – Built it Just for Us

(Pre-Chorus)
Please Just Notice Me
Give Me Just One Chance
I Will Be So Good For You
You'll Never Have To Look For Love Again

(Chorus)
Love Baby Love
That's What I Have For You
Love Baby Love
You Need It I Can Tell
Love Baby Love
Give Into It – It Will Never Stop
Love Baby Love
You Can Look Everywhere
And Never Find One So True
Love Baby Love
That's What I Have For You

High With Me (Demo Version)

Life is Very-Hard
Life is Very-Sad
All-Around is Pain and Misery
Making-Life – Seem-Not so Special
You-Can – Accept-This as Truth
Letting-Yourself – Sink-Down-Low

You're-All by Yourself – Not-Searching
For-Any-Love to Fill-Your – Heart-Up
You-Can – Stay-Like-This
Or – You-Can-Say – Like-I-Do
No-Way – Not-Me – I-Have-Love
I-Want to Give-It to Somebody
In-Hopes – They'll-Give-Me
Their-Love – In-Return
To-Fall – In-Love-With – Forever

(Chorus)
Baby I'm So Very High
You're So Very Low
I Love You A Lot Baby
But I Need A Lover
That Wants To Be
High With Me

When-We-First-Met – Baby-You-Were
The-One – That-Was so High on Life
I was Dragging with My-Shoes-Untied
You-Stopped and Tied-Them for Me
Giving a Warm-Spark to My-Lonely-Heart
That's-Been so Very-Cold – For so Very-Long

Now-That-I-Look at You-Baby
I-Can't-Help to Notice – You've-Changed
The-Warmth of Your-Being
Has-Slowly – Started to Turn-Cold
Leaving-You – Looking-Like – You're-Not in Love
And-Baby – This is Tearing – Me-Apart-Inside

(Chorus)
Baby I'm So Very High
You're So Very Low
I Love You A Lot Baby
But I Need A Lover
That Wants To Be
High With Me

Baby-I'm-Ok – Baby-I'm-Fine
I-Love-Life – I-Will-Go-On
You-Don't-Have to Worry
I-Can-Be – By-Myself-Again
I-Won't-Sink – Back-Down to No-Love
I'm-Saying to You – Pretty-Baby
I-Know-What-You – Have on Your-Mind
It's-Ok – You-Don't-Love-Me – Anymore

Don't – Feel – Bad
We-Gave-It a Shot – It-Was-Great
Because of Time – Our-Love
Simply-Faded-Away to Just a Liking
So-Dry-Your-Eyes and Give-Me a Hug

Let's-Look – Into-Each-Other's-Eyes
And-With the Past-Love – For-One-Another
Let's-Say-Goodbye as Friends
That's-What's – Best for Us
I-Hope-You-Find the Love
That-You-Deserve and Deserves-You

(Chorus)
Baby I'm So Very High
You're So Very Low
I Love You A Lot Baby
But I Need A Lover
That Wants To Be
High With Me

Lady From Space (Lyrical Story Version)

I-Know-Her-Name
It is Krie
I-Can-Understand-Her
While-She is Talking to Me
But-I-Can't – Understand-Why
For-Whom – I'm-Talking-With
Is a Lady-From-Space

She's-Dresses in Such a
Pretty-Looking – Space-Dress
Looking so Sweet and Nice
With-Her – Purplish-Pink-Skin
Smelling so Nice and Different
From-Her – Spaced-Out-Perfume

Krie – Tells – Me
She is Looking for Love
In-Need of a Hero
And-Not-Interested in Having-Sex
I-Tell-Krie – I'll-Try
I'm-Only-Human – And
She is Such a Beautiful-Space-Lady

Krie is So-Lonely and Sad
I-Invite-Her to My-Home
She-Thanks-Me by Kissing-My-Cheek
I-Make-Us – Some-Tea and Coffee
Krie-Can't-Help-Herself – She-Tries-Both
After – She-Tells-Me – Her-Story

(Chorus)
She's Not From Around Here
She's A Lady From Space
Soaring Through The Universe
On A Quest To Find A Hero
That She Can Fall In Love With

Out of a Fantasy-Novel
I am Told of a Dying-Father
With a Ruthless – Ugly-Suitor
That-Wants – Her-Father's-Land
And-Krie as His-Property
To-Enjoy – For-His-Nasty-Lust

Krie-Escaped in Search of a Hero
Her-Ship was Being-Attacked
When-She-Flew into a Black-Hole
It-Came – Out of Nowhere
Swallowing – Up-Her-Ship
This-Lady from Space
Drifted in and Out of Many-Portals
Until-Her-Ship was Finally-Released

Wouldn't-You-Know-It
Landed-Right-Here – On-Earth
Krie's-Planet is Named-Flith
Where the Inhabitants – All are Vegetarians
That-When-They – Eat the Vegetation
They-Become the Color – They-Consume

All-Over-Flith are Many-Different
Kinds of People that Consists
Of-All the Different – Kinds of Colors
That-Flith-Provides for Them to Eat
They-Become-Part of The-Land
Living-Free to Do-Everything
Living-Free to Do-Nothing at All
Because – There-Was-No-Evil
All-Colors – Were-Loved and Needed

(Chorus)
She's Not From Around Here
She's A Lady From Space
Soaring Through The Universe
On A Quest To Find A Hero
That She Can Fall In Love With

With-Tears in Her-Eyes – Krie
Continues-Telling-Me – Her-Story
Of-Such-Beauty and Such-Horror

One-Sad-Day – Evil-Landed
Thousands of Flithins-Died
For the First-Time in Their-History
They-Had to Discover – What-War-Is
Trying to Make-Weapons
They-Did-Not – Have a Chance in Using
Bullets-Killed – All-Those-That
Picked-Up – Sticks and Stones

Everywhere on Flith – Her-People
We're-Gathered-Up – And
Locked-Into – Too-Tight of Cages
The-Evil-Aliens – Wanted-Something
To-Make it Easier for Them
To-Communicate – With the Populace
They-Used – Their-Technology
A-Gas was Dispersed – Everywhere
Knocking – Everyone – Unconscious

Many-Did-Not – Wake-Back-Up
Mostly the Old and Very-Young
Those-That-Did – Now
Had a Way to Understand
To-Talk to The-Evil-Aliens
They-Learned – What-Was-Wanted
All of Flith's-Gold – That-Could be Had

(Chorus)
She's Not From Around Here
She's A Lady From Space
Soaring Through The Universe
On A Quest To Find A Hero
That She Can Fall In Love With

Understanding – What the Evil-Aliens
Wanted and Needed is Something
Very-Important for Flithins
Unfortunately – Flithins-Had-No
Understanding of Wealth
But-Learned-Real-Quickly – How-Easy
It-Is to Become – Attracted to It

Life-On-Flith – Became-Hard for Most
A-Few of The-Now – Privileged-Flithins
Had-Life on Flith – Easier on Them
For-They-Sold-Out – Their-Brethren
To the Highest-Bidder – The-Evil-Aliens

Flith the Sweet-Planet – That-Loves-Life
And-Every-One of Her-Children
Was-Now – Being-Ripped-Apart
By-Giant-Machines – That-Dig-Deep
Down-Inside-Her – Making-Her
Bleed – Scream and Cry

For the First-Time – Once-Again
Flith and Flithins – Experienced
Something-New – That was so Different
Discovered – New-Concepts-Like
Greed – Hate – Jealousy and Intense-Pain

All-Was-Lost as Flithins
Were-Made to Help-Out
By-Working – Themselves to Death
Their-Bodies – Were-Removed
As-Another – Captive-Flithin
Is-Set-Loose to Take – Their-Place

(Chorus)
She's Not From Around Here
She's A Lady From Space
Soaring Through The Universe
On A Quest To Find A Hero
That She Can Fall In Love With

93

(Spoken)

Our maybe Hero, sees this is getting heavy on Krie, so he stands up and reaches out his hand and they go for a walk. Krie loves Earth but is so sad for us as well, that Mankind uses their Planet for their gain. Our maybe hero who's name is Keith, is getting hungry so he asks Krie if she would like for him to make her the biggest Earth salad of Earth salads? Krie likes lettuce, carrots, broccoli and all other leaf and root types of vegetation. But when it comes to peppers and especially tomatoes, well the look of what kind of Nasty thing are you feeding me comes to Krie's face. Keith laughs at this which makes Krie smile and loosen up a little, just what Keith wanted for her, she's so stressed out.

This lyrical story continues after Krie and Keith take another walk but this time it is a walk under star light. Friends become a little closer as they share a single kiss, Krie shakes her head no and pulls away from Keith. Krie looks ashamed as she is staring at the ground, Keith told himself not to try anything just be a Friend, he feels ashamed as well.

(Conversation)

"I'm Sorry," Keith says. Krie looks at Keith and says, "You have nothing to be sorry about. Your Kiss is the best thing I have felt in Years. I would love to Make Love to you Keith but if I do it would help me let go of my anger and that is all I have left. I am so tired of this whole thing I just want it to stop so I can just stop being so twisted into knots inside, my head feels like is about to burst." " Krie, I would like to help you but I don't know what I can do for you. I'll be your friend, you can live with me and I'll take care of you but other than that, I have no way of helping you free your planet from its Tyranny." Krie looks at Keith and says, "Keith, you are the chosen one. A seer from one of the planets that I visited in my search of a Hero, before the black hole swallowed me up, told me that a very special, very different looking male named Keith from a planet far away was waiting for me to find him. Your name's so Strange to me, never have I heard it before and once I did, I never forgot it. In search of you, I fell in Love with you many times, hoping that there you would be just waiting for me while I was trying to keep myself safe from getting captured or killed." " I don't know what to say about that Krie, I am no Hero or warrior." " Let's go back to your home Keith and I'll finish my story. Maybe by telling you the rest, something will awaken inside you and you will become the Hero that you never thought you'd be." (Keith agrees just in time for this lyrical story to continue.)

94

Years-Have-Passed – So-Many
Flithins – Have-Passed-Died
All-In the Search for Gold
Through-These-Years
Some-Laxing-Happened
Where a Very-Pretty – Lady
Like-Krie – Could-Walk-Up
To an Airfield and Talk-Her-Way
Into-One of the Space-Ships

She-Befriended – One of the Evil-Aliens
Having-Him – Unknowingly-Teach
Krie the Basics at First – Then-Beyond
Krie-Bided-Her-Time – Learning
Until the Day – She-Escaped to Freedom

Krie's-Father was Getting-Sicker
Even-One of the Privileged-Flithins
Still-Have to Die by Normal-Means
Krie's-Father was Dying of a Broken-Heart
Because-He – Gave-Up the Position
Of a Group of Rebel-Flithins
In-Return – He was Given – Some-Land
That-He and His-Family – Could-Live-On
Free and Unharmed – Even-Protected

Everything was Going to Plan
Until a Very – Ugly-Prince
Took a Fancy to Krie – One-Day
Watching-Her – Walk-Around the Airfield
His-Fancy – Became-Reality – When
He-Showed-Up on Krie's-Land
Telling-Her and Her-Family
That-Krie-Belonged to Him-Now
And so Does – Their-Land

(Chorus)
She's Not From Around Here
She's A Lady From Space
Soaring Through The Universe
On A Quest To Find A Hero
That She Can Fall In Love With

Too-Many-Days and Too-Many-Times
Left-Krie – Almost-Without-Hope
Then the Day – Came-When
Her-Ugly-Prince – Took-His-Eyes
Off-Her – Long-Enough for Krie
To-Steal – One of the Smaller-Ships

Now-All the Past-Days – Led to This-One-Day
As-Keith-Follows – Krie to Her-Stolen – Space-Ship
Upon-Entering – Keith-Feels a Deja-Vu
Come-Crawling-Up – His-Soul and Into-His-Mind
In-Mere-Minutes – Keith-Almost-Knows-All
Of this Space-Ship and What it Could-Do

In a Few-Days-Time – Keith has Untied – His-Life
Here on Earth – Quitting-His-Job
Telling-His-Family and Friends-Goodbye
Still-Not-Feeling – Like a Hero
With-No-Battle-Plan – In-His-Mind
Keith-Starts-Up the Stolen-Space-Ship
With a Heading of Very-Far-Away

Space is Cold – Silent and Lonely
The-Two-Paired-Up – Planet-Seekers
Have – Become – Lovers
After-Months of Long-Lonely-Traveling
The-Loneliness – Became too Much

As a Kiss – Became-Another-Kiss
Which-Became a Longer-Kiss
Until the Two-Space – Traveling-Friends
Could-Not-Help-Themselves – Any-Longer
Letting-What – Both-Secretly-Been-Wanting
Have its Way as They-Fell in Love

(Chorus)
She's Not From Around Here
She's A Lady From Space
Soaring Through The Universe
On A Quest To Find A Hero
That She Can Fall In Love With

Almost a Year has Passed-By
Still-No-Sight of Planet-Flith
Keith-Misses-Earth and His-Family
But-His-Love for Krie – Makes-Him-Go-On
Then-Out of Nowhere a Black-Hole – Appears
Krie with Screams of Finally
With-Added-Tears in Her-Eyes
Pleads-Keith to Fly – Into the Black-Hole

The-Black-Hole is Very-Unstable
Making the Space-Ship – Spin-Out of Control
Keith with Quick-Wits – Brings the Ship
Back-Under-Control – Just in Time
So-They-Could-Escape – Their-Monster

The-Ship – In the Worst for Wear
Is-Leaking-Fuel and Coming-Apart
With-No-Choice – Keith-Finds a Planet
And-Lands-Their-Home – On the Ground of It
Not the Best of Landings – Cripples the Ship
The-Two-Star-Crossed – Lovers are Trapped
On a Beautiful – Green-Planet
Where-No – Humanoids-Live

There are Many – Types of animals
With-Lots of Vegetation and Drinking-Water
But-No-One to Live-With or Talk-To
They-Are-Totally – By-Themselves
The-Adam and Eve – On a Planet
That-Was-Not – Made for Them
They-Christened the Green-Planet
The-Same-Name as Their-First-Child
A-Beautiful-Girl – Named-Hope

(Chorus)
She's Not From Around Here
She's A Lady From Space
Soaring Through The Universe
On A Quest To Find A Hero
That She Can Fall In Love With

Something Extra From All Eight Sides

Big Time Love
Is Like A Beautiful Rose
With Loving Tenderness
It Blossoms And Grows

The Sun Will Shine
When I Make You Mine
The Day Will Start
When You *Catch My Heart*

Let's Be Truthful
You're So Very *Beautiful*
It's My Plan
To Always Be Your Man

They Never Know The Reason
For Whatever The Season
They're *The Lovers of Forever*
Always Bound To Be Together

Love High Flies
On Butterfly Wings
Soaring Through The Skies
Pulling At Your Heart Strings

Ladies Love – That I Can Walk The Talk
When I Close The Door
I Leave Them Begging For More
Of My Sweet Lovin' *Pillow Talk*

Her Pretty Face – Her Fine Body
Makes Me Smile
When She Takes Off Her Clothes
She *Makes Me Smile* Even More

The Lady From Space
Came To Earth To State Her Case
Looking For A Hero And Love
Leaving With High Expectations
Receiving A Little Hope

(06/08/2016) Hello, Mind Rockers. Fate? A new cover was what I desired for this book, with some thinning and some adding to the forty songs in these two books, until a thought came to my mind, "The Day After". This undiscovered day turned into eighty days later with the new song, "You Came Back To Me (85 Days Later)". This Song is sad, not what I was planning for it to be. I was singing and typing along trying to come up with something up-beat and sexy-fun but nope sad came pushing itself up front telling me here I am, use me, so I did. Finished, I continued on first by inserting my new song into its place after "Push Me Away". I finished with "Somebody Loves Me", I said another new song would be great placed here. Once again I wanted up and happy but even sadder came out. I almost said love this song and tossed it out for it was way too sad. Then I looked at it, then I sang it, then I sang it with the full passion of the lyrics. Love it, I had to keep it, so sad but so powerful, a song to remember. I finished "Catch My Heart", I said to myself, hey Man what the Love are you going to come up with next, when you create a new version of (C.M.H.) and "Catch My Soul" came to my mind. Sad once again but this time with some attitude of half/hard humor in the mix. I laughed, telling myself to let come what may and I followed my own advice.

Fast forward a little bit, I finished taking out some of the original versions of these songs and turned them into Demo Versions for the end of this book while at the same time replacing the originals with new updated 2016 versions of them. I was going to leave the Demo Versions as they are then I thought why not 2016 love them up a little bit by showing you my fans how I sing them with all the breaks in place. I now had five new songs added to Book Three and three new songs and one new bonus song added to Book Four. I said no that won't do so I created two more new songs for Book Four and said I'm done. I looked back over my ten newly added songs and noticed on Book Three, side three had no new songs added to it, the same as side four of Book Four. I laughed at the coincidence in my mind that I did not add songs to the sides that are the same number of its book. I looked at the songs on side three and decided on "Love" and thus came "I'm In Love". Side four I created "Let Me Turn You On", for it and said love it one last time and added "I'm Not Afraid Of Love" to Book Three and "Sexy Bodies (Look At That Sexy Body)" to Book Four.

I had a great time re-working these two books, even finding places for the sad songs. Books Nine and Ten are on my list to do next, I can't wait. Then it will be on to Book Eight with its trip to the dark side, with its daring me to change it, don't worry, I got it. Peace to you. The Gemini One.

www.ingramcontent.com/pod-product-compliance
Lightning Source LLC
Chambersburg PA
CBHW070224140626

46555CB00018B/1261